OUT VISITING AND BACK HOME

OUT VISITING AND BACK HOME

RUSSIAN STORIES ON AGING

Selected, Edited, and Translated by
Thomas H. Hoisington

Northwestern University Press
EVANSTON, ILLINOIS

Hydra Books
Northwestern University Press
Evanston, Illinois 60208-4210

All stories originally published in Russian: Vasily Belov, "The Burial Ground" ("Kholmy") and "That Kind of War" ("Takaia voina"), in Belov, *Takaia voina* (Moscow: Sovetskaia Rossiia, 1989). Denis Dragunsky, "Out Visiting and Back Home" ("V gostiakh i doma"), *Oktiabr'* 12 (1989). Friedrich Gorenstein, "Making the Rounds with the Shopping Bag" ("S koshelochkoi"), *Sintaksis* 10 (1982); copyright © 1982 by Friedrich Gorenstein. Nina Katerli, "The Profitted Land" ("Zemlia bedovannaia"), *Iskusstvo Leningrada* 3 (1989). Anatoly Kim, "Double Star" ("Dvoinaia zvezda"), in Kim, *Vkus terna na rassvete* (Moscow: Molodaia gvardiia, 1985). Vladimir Makanin, "One Old Man" ("Pro odnogo starika"), in Makanin, *Povest' o Starom Poselke* (Moscow: Sovetskii pisatel', 1974). Ludmila Petrushevskaya, "'Waterloo Bridge'" ("'Most Vaterloo'"), *Novy Mir* 3 (1995). Vasily Shukshin, "I Wanna Live" ("Okhota zhit'"), in Shukshin, *Tam, vdali* (Moscow: Sovetskii pisatel', 1968). Tatyana Tolstaya, "My Dear Shura" ("Milaia Shura"), in Tolstaya, *"Na zolotom kryl'tse sideli . . ."* (Moscow: Molodaia gvardiia, 1987). Ludmila Ulitskaya, "March Second of *That* Year" ("Vtorogo marta togo goda"), in Ulitskaya, *Bednye rodstvenniki* (Moscow: Slovo, 1994). Compilation and "In Place of an Introduction" copyright © 1998 by Northwestern University Press. Published 1998. All rights reserved.

Printed in the United States of America

ISBN 0-8101-1470-4

Library of Congress Cataloging-in-Publication Data

Out visiting and back home : Russian stories on aging / selected, edited, and translated by Thomas H. Hoisington.
      p. cm.
      "Hydra books."
      ISBN 0-8101-1470-4 (alk. paper)
      1. Short stories, Russian—Translations into English. 2. Russian fiction—20th century—Translations into English. 3. Aging—Russia (Federation)—Fiction. I. Hoisington, Thomas H.
PG3286.O89 1998
891.73'0108354—dc21
                                        97-48552
                                           CIP

The paper used in this publication meets the minimum requirements of the American National Standard for Information Sciences—Permanence of Paper for Printed Library Materials, ANSI Z39.48-1984.

To the memory of my grand aunt
Rena Thompson Lord
who lived to be a hundred

CONTENTS

IN PLACE OF
AN INTRODUCTION

I have been asked to describe the origins and thematics of
Out Visiting and Back Home, the collection of contemporary Russian stories on aging I selected and translated into
English. The origins are these: In 1991, near the end of a
two-year appointment researching and writing on issues
related to aging at the University of Illinois School of
Public Health, by chance I came across an age-related
story in an issue of the Russian literary journal *October,* to
which a friend in Moscow had given me a subscription.
While commuting to work on the el, I read the contribu-
tions in the "young writers" section and found Denis
Dragunsky's "Out Visiting and Back Home." This sensitive
story portrays a retired Russian VIP—a once high-pow-
ered research scientist—who is miserable because his
career has ended, leaving him with a mixture of sweet
and bitter memories. While the circumstances depicted
seemed at first distinctively "Soviet," that is, a once powerful man of the research establishment deeply troubled
by the weaknesses of his progeny, the protagonist's mus-
ings struck a familiar chord. *Americans,* not Russians,
seem more prone to complain about their offspring's lack
of success.

I began translating Dragunsky's story and resolved to search for other examples of first-rate contemporary Russian short fiction that would reflect as broadly as possible a spectrum of views on the aging process, views that would be both familiar and unfamiliar to Western readers. I knew, for example, that it was unlikely that any Russian story would include mention of a nursing home, much less of long-term care, the term favored by gerontologists and social workers in the West, because the notion of housing old people who are no longer self-sufficient in a nursing facility is alien to the way Russians think about aging relatives. Old people's homes and nursing homes, not to mention retirement villages or assisted-living residences, are virtually nonexistent. Older persons in Russia are expected to contribute to society and to the well-being of their families, with whom they often live. On the other hand, I knew that expressions and instances of prejudice against older persons by young and middle-aged Russians could be as severe, or even more severe, than in Europe and in the English-speaking world, and that even after seventy-plus years of supposedly benevolent, all-embracing institutional policies in terms of health and welfare, old people are marginalized in Russia to a much greater degree than they are in the West. With the help of Russian friends and of specialists in contemporary Russian fiction, I eventually gathered some twenty different stories by various authors on the theme of aging.

Almost without exception, Russian friends, when asked about modern stories on the subject of aging, supplied the titles of sentimental tales in which old women and men suffer out the last years of their lives dependent on family members and government bureaucrats who are indifferent, neglectful—even hostile. Though much less prone to deny that they are growing older, Russians have a much narrower view of aging than we do in the West. "Old age is no joy" (*starost' ne radost'*) is a Russian proverb one hears often. The fundamental idea, generally accepted in the West, of aging as a *lifelong* process, or, to turn it around, of life as a series of aging processes, is hard for Russians to grasp. (The friend in Moscow, a physicist by training and computer specialist by trade, whose help in obtaining writers' permissions to translate these stories was invaluable, is so baffled by what he considers "my" definition of aging that he once declared that any fiction would qualify for the collection!) Yet, as these stories attest, Russian writers reveal an understanding of aging in this broader sense and sensitively explore its many ramifications. Most of the eleven stories finally selected for *Out Visiting and Back Home* were chosen by reading a variety of short works recommended by authors rather than by translating the specific titles supplied me. A translation fellowship from the National Endowment for the Arts enabled me to devote substantial time to this project and to meet with Dr. Paulina Lewin in Cambridge, Massachusetts, on whom I rely for accuracy in my translations.

The collection that resulted offers, I believe, first-rate works addressing the broad topic of aging in ways we can profit from as well as identify with. At the same time these stories shed light on the Russian (and Jewish) experience in the late Soviet period. Friedrich Gorenstein's "Making the Rounds with the Shopping Bag," told from the viewpoint of a solitary, mouselike old woman, is an allegorical treatment of the harsh realities of urban life for the elderly in the Marxist Soviet state. Nina Katerli's "Profitted Land" looks simultaneously at age-old Russian-Jewish antagonisms and old-age dependency in two men who are both very alike and very different. Vasily Belov's "That Kind of War"—the reference is to World War II—and "The Burial Ground," and Vasily Shukshin's "I Wanna Live," raise disquieting questions about deprivation, middle-age angst, and intergenerational conflict. In the stories of both these writers, the setting is vast rural Russia. Vladimir Makanin's old man (in "One Old Man") is zany in repellent ways, whereas Ludmila Petrushevskaya's and Tatyana Tolstaya's socially marginalized female protagonists (in "'Waterloo Bridge'" and "My Dear Shura") are zany in appealing ways. Anatoly Kim's "Double Star" is a remembrance of a past relationship from two perspectives, one male, one female, that proceeds boldly beyond death (or does it?), and Ludmila Ulitskaya's "March Second of *That* Year" contrasts the onset of puberty to old age and death, the maturing of a young Jewish girl to the dying of her great-grandfather, a simple cobbler, in the frightening context of postwar Stalinist terror (the title refers to the eve of the Russian dictator's demise).

Out Visiting and Back Home is indicative of both the variety and the high quality of contemporary Russian fiction. It also is indicative of how Russian fiction has changed in recent years as a whole range of possibilities has opened up. The collection includes the work of insiders and outsiders, or, to put it another way, of outsiders who have become insiders. While Belov and Makanin were both part of the literary establishment in the Soviet period, the four women writers—Katerli, Petrushevskaya, Tolstaya, and Ulitskaya—have begun publishing only since the recent political changes in Russia. It should be noted that women writers play an important role in the literary life of the new Russia. Gorenstein, once a leading underground writer, has emigrated and lives in Berlin. His fiction is now being published in Russia. All of the writers presented here are living except for Shukshin, who died prematurely of a heart attack.

To recreate the voices of ten different authors in English has been no small task. Kim's serenely poetic, otherworldly, and dialogueless prose has an Eastern quality, reflecting his Korean heritage. Belov's style evokes sounds, smells, as well as sunlight and summer heat, whereas the story of his fellow "Village" prose writer Shukshin is filled with colloquial, earthy dialogue. A slightly ironic tone pervades the works of Makanin, Tolstaya, and Petrushevskaya. First-person storytellers are employed by Makanin and Tolstaya, while Katerli, Petrushevskaya, Ulitskaya, and to a degree Dragunsky prefer the more traditional—and detached—omniscient narrator.

All in all, *Out Visiting and Back Home* is designed to acquaint English-speaking readers with the best in contemporary Russian short fiction and to give them varied insight into the aging process not as an abstraction belonging to gerontologists, but as a complex of mental and physical changes all of us detect in ourselves as we inevitably mature and grow older.

Thomas H. Hoisington

OUT
VISITING
AND
BACK
HOME

DENIS DRAGUNSKY

OUT VISITING
AND BACK HOME

It was taking the old man a long time to die, but he wasn't suffering, he had no special ailments. He was simply expiring. His heart didn't work well anymore, nor did his kidneys. Now he'd look extremely thin, then he'd become puffy again. His left eye would become cloudy, and a thin, threadlike red vein would appear in it and then disappear. But nonetheless his thinking remained clear.

The old man was looked after by his grandson and granddaughter. His wife had been dead for a long time and his only son had died, as had his daughter-in-law, his son's wife, so only the grandchildren were left, and they took turns looking after him. Well, to say that they looked after him is going too far. They would wipe off the dust, take care of his wash, bring him newspapers, give some thought to his meals. The grandson brought him dinners in a lunch pail, and the granddaughter, when it was her turn, got them ready there on the spot. That's the sum total of what they did.

Thank God, the old man went to the bathroom on his own. He even bathed himself in the tub. So you can understand, since he could do these things himself, he didn't really burden his family too much. It was just fine if they didn't bother to drop in on him every day. Even every other day was too often. About two times a week was all that was really needed, just to make sure he was still among the living. If they wanted to ride over every day, that was up to them. He wasn't forcing them to come by every day, but he didn't drive them away either, understand. Interestingly enough, neither the granddaughter's husband nor the grandson's wife came to see him. The devil take them, a lot he cared. But at the same time he was forever being told that they didn't feel well. The old man, showing his contempt, would ask disapprovingly just how old were these citizens who ailed so. The old man did this not so much to boast about his own health, but out of scorn for those around him who were weak and puny. He regarded his balding grandson, who smoked and had a heavy, unhealthy cough, with disdain. "He should quit smoking, he's such a weakling for God's sake," the old man thought irritably. He himself almost never smoked now. Well, three puffs once a week with a small cup of coffee. Coffee, too, he now only drank once a week, no more. He'd smoked strong cigarettes since he was seventeen. Went through a pack a day and was none the worse for it. His chest was like a barrel, and his lungs, hey, they were robust! Never coughed. Nothing like that weakling. And the granddaughter was no better. She was bent over, she smoked, coughed, had a gray complexion, rings under her eyes. Once in a while, she'd come with the children, two boys and a girl, and the old man would look with displeasure at his great-grandchildren who were trying to keep quiet on the other side of the French door. He couldn't remember their names. They had names that sounded alike . . . Lyosik? Tosik? Stasik? They were also pale, anemic. His granddaughter talked all the time on the phone about pediatricians. There were endless consultations at research institutes, medical school departments. "Nothing is good enough for them," grumbled the old man to himself. "An ordinary physician won't do. They've got to have a specialist, a professor, Lord! If this is what they've got to have at age five, what'll happen when they're grown up? Will members of the Academy of Medical Sciences have to treat them?"

The old man recollected that he first had recourse to a doctor when he was about fifty, and he was really quite proud of himself for this. He had the gloomy thought that his grandson might well die before he did and how that would force him to get up, talk things over with his physician, send for a nurse, take a long time dressing, hire a cab, go buy flowers, and so on.

This reminded him of the time he buried his son. His doctor had forbidden him to go to the funeral and get worked up. What nonsense that was. After all . . . though he hadn't seen much of his son during his last years, really only on holidays, and these encounters hadn't brought him much joy. Well, so what? Mind your own business! They'd all made way for him, and so he stood by the coffin, looked, and wondered at how this dead elderly man with the flat mouth ringed by heavy folds flowing down toward his neck had been his son. Naturally, one had to weep, but who was there to weep with? He'd buried his wife long ago. So, with a face that kept growing darker, leaning heavily on his walking stick—the heavy one with the bumpy horn knob—the old man stood through the entire funeral service. Nearby, to the left and back a little, stood a pretty nurse who watched him anxiously, an oil-skin bag ready in her hand. In the doorway stood his driver plus a man named Arkady Pavlovich, broad shouldered and well-behaved.

It had now been some twenty years since the old man had the right to a driver, much less to an Arkady Pavlovich, for the old man's work had ceased to be the object of special government concern and protection some twenty years ago. However, he could summon the nurse at any hour of the day and a good doctor also, and that at least was something.

The walking stick now stood upright, leaning against the windowsill next to his desk, and the old man himself lay on the sofa in a light-colored shirt, fresh as always, and soft flannel pants with a light woolen lap robe covering him. He would stick out his large feet in their warm socks from under the lap robe, wiggle his toes gently, and thank fate for the fact that he was dying so well. First of all, it was happening at an advanced old age, and second, he had a sound mind and a good memory. But the important thing, even though it sounds funny, is that he was dying as a healthy person. It was simply time for him to die. The old man even knew how this would happen: one fine day, today in the morning or perhaps a year from now, he would simply gasp, shudder, and that would be all. A good death, though the old man was a little tired of waiting for it.

He became troublesome. He would seat his grandson or granddaughter in the easy chair next to his sofa, and say resentfully that he'd stayed just a little too long on this earth and that this state of affairs, to be honest, bored him. In general, he considered himself a visitor on this earth. He was a visitor in its vale of tears, and somehow he'd stayed too long. Homeward, homeward—to the better half of mankind! The old man recalled a well-known gravestone inscription: "I'm home, but you're just visiting." He also wanted to have a tombstone with this very same inscription as an epitaph. Moreover, he decided to take upon himself all the inevitable funeral arrangements that lay ahead. He knew that he would be given an official funeral, paid for by the appropriate offices, but he also knew how such things in fact were done. Several times he himself had been chairman of burial committees for various middle-level figures. Yes, indeed, of middle-level persons. The old man knew his exact place on the social ladder. They paid all the bills, but no more. Everything else the family had to arrange. The members of the burial committee would make an appearance only to be part of the honor guard. Everything really depended on what kind of relatives you had. . . . Looking at his grandson, the old man could picture quite clearly how, stooped over, his grandson would make his way to the counter window of the funeral office, how, stammering, he'd grope for words, and how they would send him somewhere else. He'd do all this clumsily, absurdly, not as it ought to be done, all the while perspiring out of shame and fear . . . and this filled the old man with great disgust. Consequently, the old man himself was arranging all that needed to be done and having papers drawn up, including payment for a bus.

There had to be a separate monument. Having his

name carved on his wife's stone would not do, and to add it to the stone of his son and daughter-in-law would be stupider still. Not a large stone, but a separate one, with those same words: "I'm home, but you're just visiting." The old man called in various sculptors and architects to choose the design for his monument. Ordinary gravestone carvers came, as did genuine master craftsmen, but nothing pleased the old man. The designs were all insipid, vulgar, tasteless, and so he demanded other artists, young and creative ones, to come to him. Only the most daring!

The grandson and granddaughter dealt with all his whims without complaint, but in this resignation of theirs the old man sensed concealed reproach, and that infuriated him. He was about to pose for a sculptor for a bas-relief in bronze, and then what do you suppose occurred to him? Not to have any likeness, but to have a mirror set in the stone. Wouldn't that be a meaningful hint to the pausing passerby? For whom does the bell toll? It tolls for you! But then the old man decided that this might turn out to be too fanciful. No one would understand, and then, too, the mirror might crack; or suppose some posh lady attending a large funeral used his monument to put on lipstick and brush her hair? Then a whole line of such ladies would form just as they did at the hat check in a restaurant, jostling one another in front of the mirror and stretching out their necks.

The old man loved restaurants. He liked their relaxed, lively atmosphere. He liked to take his seat at the best table. He liked to start by unfolding and spreading out his napkin shaped like a little boat and, pushing aside the menu offered by the waiter, to say, "Well then, now," ponder for a moment, gazing beyond the waiter's deferential figure, and finally announce: "Good! Now bring us . . ." He reminisced about the time when he and his son were still on good terms and would go together to dine at the Savoy or At the Tartars. (The old man loved to call restaurants by their old names.) Yes, indeed, on those fine occasions his son would marvel, "Once again you've ordered without consulting the menu. What if they don't have it?" "They'll have it, they'll have it." Not once had it happened that they hadn't had what he asked for. And even in recent times, when lines would form at restaurants, when the eternal "No Free Tables" sign hung in the door windows, the old man was let in just the same. For him a place was always found. All he had to do was take his walking stick, knock on the glass door with the knob, and the doorman would open up immediately with a smile and a small bow. Some would marvel, thinking he was known in every single food and drinking establishment. Well, some places knew him, and some places didn't. That wasn't what counted. The doorman, looking through the glass, saw by his contour, by his bearing, that a man of stature had arrived, an habitué, a person powerful and generous, and he therefore felt compelled to open the door, take the man's fur coat, call the maître d', and then reverently hand the man of stature a check for his coat. All this was done with a smile, with a slight lisp and a ready hand, into which the old man, without a glance, stuck a low-denomination note.

"How little it takes to make others bow and scrape before you," thought the old man with quiet scorn. How little—presence, a firm voice, a penetrating glance, and that unquestioning announcement after a moment of thought: "Well then, now!" Thus he didn't care for people who were ready to yield, to dust themselves off, to hold their tongue, to smile obsequiously. In general, he felt alien amidst this worried, frightened tribe. In a word, he felt like a visitor. Yes, yes, indeed, just a visitor. He'd lived his whole life as if he were visiting. And it would have been fine if he had been visiting only on cheerful and pleasant occasions, but that wasn't the case. As if to spite him, he was forced to take part in a dull dinner party in a unrefined middle-class home where everyone smiled mawkishly and peered into each other's faces. Brrr! Oh, back home, back home. . . . He'd come to hate his son for precisely this softness, this pliable quality, for the fact that he hadn't been able at the right moment to hit the table with his fist and shout, "Well then, now, Papa!" as he in his own time had shouted at his father. Because of this, his father had allotted him a legitimate share of their trading business and let him go to Hamburg to study under Professor von Staufenberg. It was frightening to think what might have become of him had he not persisted in doing what he wanted. Thus the old man could not stand visits by his son and daughter-in-law. The son would appear at the doorstep embarrassed in advance, full of apologies. He would throw himself on his father with a kiss, and embrace his shoulders with soft, moist hands. The daughter-in-law, on the other hand, would talk very independently and also try to demonstrate her independence by sitting in an easy chair, legs crossed, jiggling a stylish shoe on her toe. The studied quality of her behavior, her supposedly daring remarks, and the supposedly casual way she sat were so pitiful that the old man was almost ready to cry out in revulsion. His son was a complete nonentity. At twenty, at thirty, and at forty-five, he was merely his father's son and nothing more—to anyone. The old man heard with his own ears a conversation in the ministry corridor: "So-and-so died. . . ." "Who's that?" "You know, the son of so-and-so." "Oh, yes. . . ." So, my boy, even when you're on the other side of the mortal boundary, you're still the son of so-and-so and nothing more, it serves you right. Why mourn about the fact that, as they say, "Alas! He died young." If a person has not been able, figuratively speaking, to carve out much of anything in fifty-two years, then why expect him to be able to do more after that? Nature is wiser. Only it's sad that no one understands that.

The old man thought that no one would understand him either. They wouldn't understand why he'd rejected official burial at government expense with great derision and decided to erect his own tombstone with such a daring epitaph. Naturally, everyone would think he was showing off, showing off, moreover, out of spite. He had the right to a state-paid funeral, yet here he was frittering away money on sculptors and stonemasons, even though he had a grandson with a child and a granddaughter with three children. He did indeed have two grandchildren and four great-grandchildren, and it's not as if they were all that well situated in life. When the grandson or granddaughter brought him dinner, did he ever ask, "Who paid for this?" To be sure, roughly once a month, he asked if they had enough money. Naturally, they replied that everything was OK. That was bad. . . .

Maybe it was not really a matter of haughty derision, but rather simply the old man's way of being difficult, of showing off. The old man himself thought about this a couple of hours, at times nodding, and then he summoned his granddaughter, ordered her to sit down, and announced that he was revoking all his decisions regarding the burial. He ordered her to take all the receipts and the informal agreement with the sculptor, get back all the money advanced, and use it for whatever she needed. The granddaughter listened, politely nodding her head and sighing to herself, because all this was simply the old man's way of being difficult, of showing off. The old man understood this too. He grew silent and soon dozed off.

He dreamed the dream he'd long wanted to dream. In it he was returning home after having been on a visit, and he was standing on a small, round stage surrounded by a huge amphitheater, his home, the abode of the greater and better half of humankind. Everyone was calling and motioning to him. He moved toward them, ascended, and they all pointed out his place. He sat down, and people leaned over the row and across the seats to embrace him, shake hands with him, pat him on the shoulder. It was all very much like a large auditorium in an old university building. In front of everyone, himself included, lay an open but full pack of cigarettes, matches, an ashtray, and also a pad of paper and a sharpened pencil. It was as if they'd all gathered for a conference. Down below, the round stage had turned into the

Earth with cities and fields, with dark blue seas and rivers, like those on a map, and people could be seen rushing about, pitiful and awkward. Up above, everyone looked at these people and noted something quickly on their pads of paper. What were they writing, and why? Oh, yes. This must be what Mama had said about his late grandfather: "Grandpa looks down at us from Heaven. He sees everything from Heaven." That's just what they were doing, looking down at their relatives and immediately recording all their mistakes and faults. The old man turned around and tried to see his grandpa, his father, his wife—and also his son and daughter-in-law. But he saw none of them. With so many people to look at, you couldn't.

In his dream, the amphitheater way up high receded and disappeared into the mist. Then the old man looked down again, to the Earth, and he caught sight of Kamenka, where he had vacationed at a dacha, and his neighbor Tanya Sadovsky. He was then a high school student. Fifteen years old. Tanya was also fifteen. They lived next door to each other. Tanya was wearing fine white stockings and shoes. She'd just arrived from the city and didn't look at all like she was on vacation, with her even part and neat round bun on the back of her head and the small round glasses with gold rims on her nose. He, on the other hand, had just emerged from the woods, wearing tarred boots and a padded jacket with a hunting rifle and two hazel grouse hanging from his belt. They had run into each other in the lane. He impulsively extended his hands to her and began to kiss her. She stood still, with her eyes shut and her head lowered. He mumbled her name and kissed her, but what kept touching his lips were the cold rims of her glasses. He kissed the glasses as well, and this must have been painful because suddenly she shook her head and looked him straight in the eye. She had gray eyes and a refined nose. She looked at him through her glasses, and he realized that he was dying of love. Before he had only read in books about someone dying of love. But now he was dying of love himself and, gazing into her eyes, which looked somehow double because of the glasses, he murmured, "Tanya, I love you. Let's get married. D'ya want to?" She half-shut her eyes and nodded slowly. Then he removed her glasses and kissed her on the lips as a bridegroom would his bride. And she embraced him, responding to his kiss, but then suddenly pulled back, grabbed her glasses from him, and fled. By the time he rushed after her, it was too late, she'd already run up onto the porch of her dacha. He pulled on the gate, which was locked, then put his hand through it and groped for the catch. But at that moment, around the house, choking on their barking, came flying Arkhar and Mastak, the famous hounds of Tanya's older brother, Kolya. From the porch Kolya himself immediately shouted, "Down! Down! Who's there?!"

The old man woke up. The barking of the dogs still rang in his ears, and he was somewhat exhausted from the chase. The lightness of a fifteen-year-old youth surged through his entire body. But this feeling subsided immediately, and he was fully awake and felt like an old, old man lying on a sofa waiting for death.

Through the glass door, the old man caught sight of his granddaughter. She was standing, talking on the telephone. Leaning on a table, she was crudely scratching the calf of her right leg with the toe of her left shoe. Out of the corner of her eye, she noticed that he'd woken up, but she continued to talk about medical tests, about a good consulting physician, an order for a health spa in Eupatoria, and other nonsense.

Doubtless, his granddaughter did not like him. And his grandson didn't like him either. For example, there was the matter of the apartment. Of course they were miffed that they lived devil-knows-where in shabby apartment buildings while he resided in elegant loneliness on Nezhdanov Street. But even more important, after his death the apartment would be gone, that is, none of them would get it, and this of course was a shame. But, reflected the old man bitterly, how was it any less shameful that here was a person dying and his closest relatives were walking around and snarling, estimating his living space. Confound it! Well, let them. Let them get official permission to live in his apartment as soon as possible. But which one should it be? His grandson or his granddaughter? Whoever. Did he have to resolve this matter for them too? They'll fight about it, sighed the old man. God, they'll really fight about it . . . and blame him for everything.

The old man was well aware that many people thought he'd driven his wife and son, and his daughter-in-law as well, to their graves with his sudden whims, his dinners in restaurants, games of Russian whist, and iron-like health. That was unfair! Didn't they realize how hard he had worked? How important his work had been? What those times had been like? Wasn't he away from home for weeks, sleeping in his laboratory? Sure, the restaurants, their noise and bands, were as necessary to him as the air we breathe. That was how he relaxed; it was his way of relieving tension, of recharging himself for future work. Sure, some catch fish, others pedal around on a bicycle. But he, pardon me, had dinner in restaurants. Pardon me again, with champagne. And, pardon me once more, in the company of nice ladies. So, after all, why did he have to account for this? Also, as far as the card games were concerned . . . anyhow, he did that at informal conferences. Many of the most serious matters were discussed around the card table. Well, OK, OK. It may well be that he was really overbearing, demanding, that he even showed off. But didn't he work for them, for the sake of his family? For he, the pupil of von Staufenberg, could easily have become a quiet university professor, quietly advancing a theory—and there would have been plenty of money and glory. But his wife had been a great beauty. They'd had a son right away. All his work and achievements, all his ranks and titles, medals and prizes—all of this was really for them, for them alone. Yet, despite all this, people thought he was a petty tyrant, an egoist, and that he'd sent them all to their graves.

The memory of Tanya Sadovsky returned suddenly to the old man. Again he felt that he was dying out of love for her as he had back then in the lane near the dachas. God, why had things turned out the way they had? If he'd married Tanya, he wouldn't have caused her to go to her grave because of restaurants, betrayals, and bad blood between them. He would have loved her, cherished and protected her. The son they produced would have been good, strong, and smart. He would have respected his father, yet been an independent person. And the grand-children would have been healthy and happy, not like these sourpusses. God, how bad everything had turned out. What a horrible mistake. His entire life had been one mistake and nothing could correct it now. But why? Why was this so?

The old man turned on his side and gazed with spite at the portrait of his wife hanging opposite the window. It had been painted in '28 in Paris by the famous Russian avant-garde painter Saul Fishman. All cubes and free-flowing designs, a pale arm, a gold pince-nez on a finely set nose. Then the old man remembered that his wife Tatyana Anatolevna was that same Tanya Sadovsky from the dacha village of Kamenka in his dream.

Why can't you live your life first as if it were an approximation, a draft, adjusting yourself to it and trying things out, and only later, knowing how and understanding what is what, really live it worthily, beautifully, and happily? But if this can't be done, why can't you in your final years at least correct all your mistakes, ask people to forgive you, show people lots of kindness, love people again? You can't, you can't, thought the old man in despair, because no one's left. If he could only tell his stories to someone. But he couldn't do this either because they wouldn't believe him, they would just laugh. You couldn't do anything . . . but why? It was so unfair, stupid, illogical. As a result, new people would also torment themselves and grieve, and only in the face of death would they understand where and how they went wrong, but they would not be able to do anything about it. They wouldn't even know how to forewarn others.

He turned again on his back and looked through the

glass door. His granddaughter was still talking on the phone. She got a cigarette, groped for a box of matches, and lit up while holding the receiver to her ear with her shoulder. She began to cough, covering the receiver with the palm of her hand. What a plain girl, thought the old man sympathetically: a shrunken chest, heavy legs, as if from inferior stock. Who from? You couldn't blame her grandpa or grandma, that's for sure. But, just the same, he felt pity for her, almost to the point of tears. It had never even occurred to the old man that he could feel sorry for this virtually alien, unattractive woman. But he very much wanted to approach her, utter something especially affectionate, stroke her head. With difficulty, he threw back the afghan, grabbed the leather-covered button on the back of the sofa—there was nothing else to grab hold of—got up, lowered his legs from the sofa, and began searching for his slippers.

Hearing his rustling, the granddaughter turned around and dropped the telephone receiver. The old man saw that she was looking at him with a changed expression on her face. Then and only then did he understand that all that recent talk of his about who was visiting and who was at home, that all this was nonsense, hogwash, rot, foolish clowning. His home was here. Here, here, here. His loved ones were also here, in his own, favorite dwelling. He didn't want to go away from here ever, not even on a visit, for the dwelling *there* was cold and unknown, and how they'd meet him there . . . only God knew.

FRIEDRICH GORENSTEIN

MAKING THE ROUNDS
WITH THE SHOPPING BAG

Old Avdotya woke up very early and immediately thought about her shopping bag. "Oh my, oh my, oh my," she began to lament. "Oh, o-oh. . . . Just yesterday when I was carrying a can of milk in it, the handle gave way. It's all worn out. If only I can manage to mend it before the stores open."

She glanced at her old, old alarm clock. There was a time when this alarm clock roused and woke up Avdotya and all the others. . . . And who were they? Well, what's the point of remembering? Does old Avdotya's biography actually have any meaning now?

A Soviet citizen remembers all the details and ramifications of his biography, thanks to the numerous forms he is forever having to fill out. However, old Avdotya hadn't filled out a form for years, and of all the state institutions her main interest was concentrated on grocery stores. For poor Avdotya was your typical grocery store old woman, the type of person not taken into account by socialist statistics but who actively takes part in the consumption of socialist goods.

Before evening, when tired working people pour out of their plants, factories, and offices and, exhausted by rush-hour public transport, squeeze into hot, gas chamber–like stores, old Avdotya will have managed to dart about everywhere, like a tiny mouse. . . . She'll have got hold of some good Bulgarian eggs there, some delicious Polish ham there, a fine Dutch chicken there, sweet-tasting Finnish butter there. You could call it food geography. The pleasant taste of a native apple from the Vladimir region or of sweet, dark-red cherries she's all but forgotten. Even the berries she picks outside Moscow are to supplement her pension and not for her own consumption.

With her handy shopping bag she'll go into those thinly wooded areas still standing as if entering a grocery store to buy tasty wild raspberries and strawberries from good old mother nature, getting there before the alcoholics who follow Michurin's advice and don't wait for what nature can provide but pick the wild raspberries to make money for drink. They clean out these meager woods so thoroughly that the birds have nothing to peck at, the squirrels nothing to chew on. After robbing nature's smaller creatures, they press down hard on the brothers and sisters of the toiling masses.

She'll sell the shopping bag full of sweet raspberries she's gathered for a ruble a shot glass and purchase a kilogram of bananas from Peru for a ruble ten per kilo. She'll sell huckleberries at a ruble fifty a shot glass and purchase Moroccan oranges for a ruble forty a kilo. Isn't life under socialism good? The fighters for peace in the West know that's the truth. 'Tis a pity only that their proof-filled propaganda campaigns do not take advantage of the balance from old Avdotya's accounts, poor old Avdotya's surplus value.

Socialism, now there's a distributor for you.

Everyone eats according to what he deserves. And there's a multitude of deserving folks under socialism. That the mouths of people belonging to the high echelons of government or to winter sports contests, or to those who have been sent into outer space, or to the members of the presidiums of the unions of creative people should be well fed is quite obvious. So they are beyond the scope of our story. Our tale is not one about those who eat, but about those who gather up the crumbs after them.

In all fairness, it should be pointed out that this is hard work. Indeed, this is where that principle of socialism, "He who does not work does not eat," is fully operative . . . except that the purpose of the work is not producing goods, but rather chasing after them. The principle, as a matter of fact, is not a new one. From time immemorial you could either buy goods or plunder them. However, during the period of mature socialism, these two methods have become one. You have to start by using sheer force to get hold of the goods and only then do you pay for them. For, after all, we are not in the woods nor are we robbers on the highways. The Nightingale-Robber of the ancient ballads would find nothing to do here. The bludgeon, the lead weight on a rope tied to a stick as a work tool would be useless here. The lead weight is now employed in the exchange of commodities—not for fracturing a skull, but to weigh and to cheat. Though a skull may be fractured if there happens to be a good "shoving" session. But more about shoving later on. You need only add that, as is the case with any job, professional experience is a must along with the observance of precautionary measures. Poor Avdotya, an old hand in the struggle for food supplies, had participated in commercial robbery for a long time. She was experienced, and the main tool of her trade was her shopping bag. Avdotya dearly loved her shopping bag. Getting ready for her workday, she'd troll, "You're a real provider, aren't you! You're like my own bossy."

Her plan had been drawn up in advance. First, go to "our" store. (That was the one next to the building where she lived.) Then to the bakery. Then to the big store with its various sections. Then to the meat store. Then to the milk store. Then to the "dealicatessen." Then to the store at the foot of the hill. Then to another "dealicatessen." Then to the store run by Tartars. Then to the vegetable stand. Then to the bakery opposite the stand. Then to the store next to the post office. . . .

This last store was bad, dangerous. There was a good chance you'd get shoved in it. People didn't indulge you there. They came from the buildings close by, part of a plant that produces articles made out of rubber. But it was right there that old Avdotya got hold of two hundred grams of delicious Tambov ham. This pleasant event occurred two weeks ago. So, perhaps she'll be lucky again. When these people shove, you have to know how to fall down—and not the way Martynovna did. She's still lying in the hospital. She was pushing her way up to a counter when she ran into a detachment of people who had come by bus from a nearby industrial suburb in search of food.

Large numbers of buses of this sort are dispatched by factory and plant committees in the towns surrounding Moscow for excursions to the cultural attractions of the capital: the Tredyakov Gallery, the sights of the Kremlin, the Bolshoi Theater. . . . The people who come are strong, broad-shouldered, or they're nimble and crafty. And armed to the teeth with all kinds of containers and shopping bags. Well-organized folks. More about cultural excursions, however, in due time. . . .

It's already late according to the alarm clock. Any moment now, the objects of attack will be opening, and old Avdotya's working day will begin. Avdotya has already got her beloved shopping bag ready, taking with her a juicy apple to munch on and her cherished vasodilating medicine in case of emergency. She has crossed herself and is on her way. . . .

She enters "our" store, and right then and there comes upon a big find: they're selling chickens. And not the frozen ones, which are like stone, but the chilled, semidressed ones. Wouldn't our Avdotya like to get a chicken like that? Of course she would, because she's old and her organism doesn't tolerate spicy, hot, or sour food. All she has to do is eat a little pickled cucumber or tomato and how she burps.

The other day she indulged herself a little and ate a pickled tomato and a potato. Then she went for a walk to get some fresh air. But very soon her old legs got tired. She sat down on a bench. Next to her were young people, a he and a she, sitting and whispering to one another. They said something to one another, then paused and kissed. He kissed and old Avdotya burped. Then once again, kiss, burp. He moved over to Avdotya and said in a whisper, "Get outta here, you old bag, or I'll knock out the rest of your teeth."

"Oh, my gosh." Did he really think he could scare Avdotya? "Oh my, oh my."

But old Avdotya was not easily scared. "I'm burping in accordance with the laws of the organism," she said, "and you're bein' rowdy and that's against the law! I'm callin' the cops."

Old Avdotya was strong, really strong. Socialism guarded her rights and protected her old age. The young folks went and finished their kissing on another bench, and Avdotya finished her burping—with its pickled tomato aftertaste.

A juicy tomato or cucumber was good, but potent. A good broth, however, would be kind to her frail old bones and make them smooth. Tender, light chicken meat doesn't make the head heavy nor does it produce diarrhea. How can Avdotya get a chicken that will help her keep up her strength, so that she won't have to yield her place in life earlier than necessary to impudent youths?

Avdotya looks the place over with an experienced eye. The line, though pretty long, is nonetheless peaceful, languid. In it stand beef-eaters. A face, the back of a head, a face, the back of a head. Avdotya moves slowly and quietly. She makes her way to the counter where chickens are being sold and looks at them lovingly. "Cluck, cluck, cluck," the old, cunning vixen Avdotya keeps repeating to herself like in the fairy tale. "I'm gonna eat this delicious chicken meat, I'm gonna get it. The beef-eaters won't be upset. I'm only gonna deprive these good people of a single chicken." There're lots of chickens right there on the counter. Which one is old Avdotya going to grab right up? Which one will end up in her shopping bag?

But then, suddenly, trouble. What bad luck and even worse disaster: the blind woman was approaching. Old

Avdotya knew this blind woman and in the battle for food avoided her. This blind woman was middle-aged or even younger, and her face was ordinary, beefy, like one of those women who spend lots of time in lines. But she was privileged. She could be oblivious to her surrounding reality, and was proud of this whenever she had to deal with people, acting as if she had been elected to public office or were a national hero. She would come in, immediately thrust herself forward, shove, shout angrily at everyone. If she only would ask or quietly move forward, no one would have minded. She wanted to play up her superiority and privileges, however, and so she'd grab a lot.

"Whatever I need, I take," she'd cry. "And if another blind person comes in, he legally can take as much as he needs. But you who can see—you can stand here until you get screwed."

She shouts and rakes chickens off the counter. Onto the scales and into her possession, onto the scales and into her possession. In her hands is not just an ordinary shopping bag but a backpack. Strong, sinewy hands. A she-wolf. That nice chicken she raked in is the very one Avdotya had picked out for herself. Avdotya is infuriated. She forgot that she herself was not in line.

"That's not legal," she shouted. "That's not legal."

This caused a stir in the line. Peaceful, it was peaceful, that line, but at home there were pots, bowls, spoons—families were waiting. Those at the end of the line began to grumble: there would be nothing left for them. Those at the head of the line were vexed as well: they'd spent two hours on their feet in stuffy air.

"It's not right," they cried out. "They should set up a

separate store for the blind, the one-eyed, and the deaf."

The blind she-wolf, however, brawled with the line. "You old witch, you're no different," she shouted back to someone.

"I'm not a she but a he," came the response.

She can't see with her eyes, and when the line is noisy you can't always distinguish men's voices from women's.

"You're a fool, woman," she shouted.

"You're the one who's the fool," was the man's answer. "But I'm a fool too for standing almost three hours on my feet."

Old Avdotya was actually to blame. Had she not begun to shout, perhaps the line would have remained quiet. Oh, what bad luck and even worse disaster. Don't go near this sort of line. Don't try to get the chicken you want by waiting in this sort of line. But all the same, the blind she-wolf did really grab too much. . . . Our Avdotya left with her shopping bag empty. She was so upset she forgot to go to the bakery, but instead went directly to the big store.

In the big store it was never calm. You dove in and waves of people picked you up and carried you along . . . from the dry foods section to the general grocery section, and from the general grocery section to the meat section. And everywhere there were elbows and shoulders, elbows and shoulders. The one good thing was that they weren't able to push you here; there was no place to fall. But a great abundance of elbows. You'd get one in the physiognomy, or why not say, without ceremony, in the *puss*.

Flat tins of herring piled on a handcart have just been

brought out. For old Avdotya, this was a piece of cake. No regular line had had time to form; it was plunder pure and simple. Whoever can grabs first. Here Avdotya didn't need the cunning of a fox but that of a mouse. It was like a circus. Now you see it, now you don't. The cart was already empty. People looked around to see who had what. Men had grabbed one or two tins. Several had grabbed only air and were standing there angry. In the lead were strong, experienced housewives who got three or four tins. Among them were a few single old women. Avdotya had three tins in her shopping bag.

On the whole, when the old food-chasing women unite, they present a terrible threat. Once, seven old women, Avdotya among them, pushed their way to the counter in single file, leaning on one another. In front was Matveevna, who is in the hospital right now with a fracture. That time she was leaning on a stafflike crutch. They scattered everyone in the line and got hold of some really tender Polish ham. To be sure, you have to size up the situation in advance. For example, take the situation now in the meat department; you shouldn't mess with it. Something has been brought out, but what exactly is not so clear. Half crush, half brawl. Some people in the crowd force a smile. These are the ones who pretend their brutality is horseplay. However, the majority of faces are serious and angry; they're doing their job.

Oh dear, you'd better leave, Avdotya. You've grabbed the herring you wanted so bad, so leave. Herring does not make a beneficial broth. It tickles as it swims through your gut and produces a painful belch. But still you crave it. You can't always eat what the doctor orders; sometimes you have to indulge yourself. A potato will take up the salt, and some good sweet tea will set things right. You've grabbed some fatty herring, so leave, Avdotya, while you're still whole. Leave, Avdotya.

However, it was one of those bad days when everything goes wrong. But when Avdotya realized what was happening, it was too late. At first you couldn't even turn around, then you could hardly breathe. Then there was a new smell: that of crude, home-grown tobacco, tar, the tar smell of the denizens of the industrial suburbs. They'd arrived. Their excursion buses were parked right next to the supermarket. Each bus served as the mobile headquarters of a food detachment. Here they brought what they'd bought by force. The bus was jammed with sacks, satchels, and string bags. The troops—strong-armed men and women—were moving in various directions. And nimble young folk made up the scouting party. A freckled girl rushed about shouting, "Uncle Parshin, Aunt Vasilchuk told me to tell you that they're selling vegetable lard."

"Now what kind of lard is that, you little fool?"

"Yellow," the freckled one nodded merrily. "I got in, looked, they're selling it. . . . But someone or other let Aunt Vasilchuk have it good with his shoulder."

But Uncle Parshin wasn't listening any longer. "Vaniukhin, Sakhnenko! Bring the milk can!"

The battle crew came running with a forty-liter can. Oh, there're so many from the industrial suburbs. Y'couldn't get through them. And, worse still, they were pushing in their big can.

"Oy, h-e-e-e-l-l-l-p me! H-e-e-e-l-l-l-p me!"

The people of the blue-collar suburbs work hard. Sausage, cheese, and various grains are tossed through the air. There's a harvest in progress. He who does not reap, neither shall he chew. And if you don't get to chew and you get the Party news sheet, you'll get angry. It's bad when ideological deviations begin in a suburban industrial zone. Suburban industrial zone? And who exactly lives there? The toughest and best fighters for Russia, that's who. "When there's enough in our stomachs, we're ready to use our cudgels against anybody. We'll spit on the bald spots of Czechs and Poles in the name of the battle for peace, so that they'll calm down. . . . There was a time when we fought with cycle chains soaked in kerosene. Now we can hit any imperialist's puss even better with tanks and rockets. All you need to do is whistle, Party Central Committee, all you need to do is shout: 'Comrades, stand from under!' However, to be left completely without food, Central Committee, is simply impossible. The industrial suburban zone is your underpinning, Our Father Central Committee, but you go 'n' feed that whore—Moscow. Though even in Muscovy vodka's not always available for refueling the organism."

There go three Moscow proletarians. The puffy one wearing glasses discusses things endlessly.

"We should call the president of the Moscow Soviet and say that there is neither vodka nor meat." (We're now in another location: the store at the foot of the hill.) "We should call the Moscow Soviet!"

From the proletarian who is a little more intelligent: "Is the president really to blame?"

"Who else? How not so? He promised to make Moscow a model city. On paper. . . . On paper. . . . On paper!!!" he cried, the third time nearly bursting.

The gray-haired proletarian, who looks like a public-spirited person, to a store worker: "Why is there nothing here?"

The store worker: "There's nothing anywhere."

"That's not true. Your store didn't put in their orders early enough. Where's the manager?"

"Go to the dry foods section. He's there." The store worker is grinning.

He went there. A Russian on his way to seek the truth. A favorite occupation. It's a long way. . . . We'll not follow him, we're following old Avdotya.

Avdotya had escaped. And she'd rescued her favorite shopping bag. Avdotya had lived a long time in this world and she was clever. She sought not truth but food products. But it was just that sort of day when all her plans went awry. She dropped into a "dealicatessen." It was quiet, peaceful there. The air was fresh and the counters were spotlessly empty. They didn't even care enough to put anything out for show. Not so much as a dog's bone. The sales clerk sat propping up her cheek with a hand. People came in, they cursed and spat. But old Avdotya went in, stood for a bit, caught her breath, and then asked: "Are there any fresh fillets of meat to be had, dearie? Or any really tender flank steak?"

"It's clear, granny, that'ya came to the wrong place," the salesgirl replied. "You don't need a deli, but an eye doctor. Don't you see what's on the counter?"

Old Avdotya didn't take offense. "Thank you," she said, "for the advice." And she proceeded to another "dealicatessen." She went in—and she found something! She managed to purchase some kidneys before a man wearing a hat got them. The kidneys were like those in a dissecting room, soaking all by their lonesome on a dish, and Mr. Swell was studying and sniffing them. He took off his glasses and put them on, off, on. Old Avdotya rushed over to the cashier and paid for the kidneys.

"How could you!" cried out the intellectual. "I was first."

"You were sniffing, but this little lady here paid for them," said the shop worker.

"Are there any more?"

"That's all. Y'can buy this delicacy instead. We have it only once in a while."

The intellectual looked at something incomprehensible. He read the label: "Caviar on Egg." He looked closer. Indeed, this was not a fresh egg but a hard-boiled one cut into halves, and on the sulphurous yolk lay black sparrow dung. "So where's the caviar?"

"That's as much as there's supposed to be. Thirty grams. How much do you expect for that price?"

That price, even under Khrushchev, who believed that the will is the primary factor of our experience, even on the eve of the historic October Party Plenum of 1964, which had produced major changes in the development of agriculture, for that price one could buy two hundred grams of good caviar in any decent grocery store. Russia advances quickly, as if it were being pursued by wild dogs. And where are we rushing to? Why not sit and rest, ponder a little, wipe the sweat from our brows. But try and say so, and the political analysts will ridicule you.

Every evening, the analysts-cum-warders peer into the cell camera, the television camera, as into a prison cell peephole. They talk about failures in the West and successes in the East. There is some success, of course, which cannot be denied. The caviar for the egg, for example, one can only weigh on an electronic scale, like elemental particles.

So reasoned the ulcerous, peevish intellectual. But old Avdotya had put the kidneys she'd paid for before him in her shopping bag—and gone on. This was all for the best. The intellectual would have thrown these kidneys into a skillet, charred them, chewed them up bitter taste 'n' all, and wolfed them down in chunks. That night you'd have had to call an ambulance for him. Old Avdotya, however, will soak these kidneys in some cold water. She will pour off the bitterness with the water and only then boil them up. They will become nice 'n' soft. Then she'll pop them into the skillet with some tasty butter, a tablespoon of flour, and also a dash of onion. If a burp comes up as a result of the kidneys, it will be a peaceful one, a delicious reminder.

So lives Avdotya, that old food-hunting woman without a biography. She has adapted. The political analyst may peer into her little television as she is treating herself to kidneys. The face of the political analyst will twist, become distorted, and he'll begin to bawl in a voice not his own, since the television has needed repairs for a long time. But what can you do? The use of fine caviar or delicious, wet-smoked sausage was forbidden by her doctor, but she still is permitted to munch on kidneys. And there are still other products that haven't yet been entirely taken away. Bountiful, bountiful Russia. In one place there's a line for Indian tea, in another a line for fine Bulgarian eggs, and in a third a line for Romanian tomatoes. Stand and it's yours.

Old Avdotya went into the milk store. A peaceful and calm product, milk, a nonalcoholic beverage. It's used by infants and people on special diets. Quiet lines are not the exception here. But not today because prepackaged Finnish butter is for sale.

Now, voices from the line should not be confused with the voice of the line. Generally speaking, sociologists have yet to thoroughly study the line as an entity. The line shapes a person's psyche, his or her attitude toward life. But how could these sociologists define old Avdotya's type of experience?

Avdotya went in and listened: the line was whining like a circular saw that has hit a stone at top speed. The line's "face" was hypertense, red and white, blood and milk in the truest sense. Avdotya slowly backed out of there and into the store of the Tartars, where a Tartar is the manager and his wife sells juice.

It's as if these Tartars were being raided by Ukrainians from the steppe . . . anarchists, the bands of Makhno. They all have the same uniform: kerchiefs and plush, double-breasted, fur-trimmed jackets. Heavy hands, purple, crimson-colored faces and garlic breath. . . .

However, of late, Russians too, especially policemen for some reason, have garlic breath. Is it from the sausage? Maybe they're trying to mask the low quality of its contents with garlic?

The Makhnovites call to one another in Ukrainian. "Teklya, where's Tern?" "Gone with Gorpyna for champagne."

If the working class from the industrial suburbs are the ones who clean out the basic items, then it's the Makhnovites who clean out the luxury items. They bring to market sacks of pumpkin seeds or early pears. They stuff the sacks with money and then into those sacks go the expensive delicacies. There's Gorpyna helping Teklya lift onto her shoulder a sack full of champagne. And there's Tern with knapsacks in both hands, stuffed with chocolate bars and boxes of chocolate candies.

It evokes memories of the partisan's tar-smeared gun carts, loaded with belongings looted from the gentry. Now, however, it's a different sort of pillage, not Bakunin's kind but Marx's: Goods—money—goods. . . .

The Soviet store epitomizes both the history and economy of the state, and its politics, its morality, and its social order.

A wooden stand. The selling of vegetables. "I'm closing up now. No service."

"You're not closing. This is a state enterprise, not a private shop. And the people standing here are part of the state too."

The best thing you can do with vegetables from state

enterprises is throw them out. But the people stand in line, hoping that not everything has been left to rot and not everything has been brought green, unripe.

A fish market. "Two nice fish."

"I'll give you two nice fish in the face."

"Slut!"

"Who?"

"Here. . . ."

"You take it."

"Go to hell!"

Let's go further. . . . Here's some other department.

"How much can you buy?"

"There still won't be enough for all of us."

"Two kilos each."

"Are you standing in line?"

"No, I'm lying in it."

"What'd you say?"

"Go to hell!"

The permanent cold war of hot smoked meat never ceases. This is where peace fighters could find ample room for their activities. This is where foreign diplomats should study problems. Get hold of a string bag, stuff it full of empty kefir and wine and vodka bottles, put on a dirty shirt, stand long enough in front of the heater to sweat, and go to the store. What you have to know is how to jostle with your elbows, stare intently, and utter a single Russian phrase: "You go to ———!"

You can fill in the rest of the phrase in your own language. Everyone understands where they're being sent. The foreigner in Russia is, however, a privileged person.

He goes to the "Beriozka" foreign currency store or to the Central Market.

At the Central Market there is an abundance of high-quality food products—and foreign makes of automobiles. The nation knows how to grow firm, sun-ripened tomatoes and cool, aromatic cucumbers, butter-soft dessert pears and fragrant peaches so beautiful that they decorate a holiday table as well as flowers. The nation knows how to display dressed, soft yellowish-white geese, ducks, hens, and turkeys on counters. There are mounds of fresh meat, chunks of lightly salted pork fat that melts in your mouth, heady-smelling fish, white cream curd cheese rich in fat, thick sour cream. . . . Here at the Central Market the New Economic Policy is still in full swing. Here there is no progressive movement toward communism, no doing more than the Plan specified, no grandiose flights into space, no fight for peace. Here the leader of the Chilean Communist Party, acquired thanks to an exchange, peacefully digs into mounds of fragrant Georgian greens, greens which remind him of those back home in Latin America.

It's great to be at the Central Market. But it's also enough to make you cry. You'd like to go up to the general secretary of the Chilean Communist Party, while he still wears the face of an agreeable cook and not that of a vicious machine gunner, and say: "Dear *Camarada* Lucio, Citizen Chairman"—we'd even flatter him, count on his vanity—"you fight to liberate the oppressed and hungry from exploitation. So as an internationalist, help old Avdotya. Take pity on Avdotya, since she cannot take good enough care of herself. She is old, sick; she has indigestion, weak eyesight, and suffers from head ailments and from other infirmities of a difficult old age, the consequence of a difficult young life. Tell your friends up there in high places, your comrades in world revolution, our own leaders, about old Avdotya. Tell them also about the fools from the industrial suburbs, because they, too, deserve pity, and about the intellectual in the hat. And even about the Makhnovites who nearly bust their guts and do in their tickers with bundles full of champagne. Don't be offended, *Camarada,* don't turn green from anger, don't distort your well-known visage as an ardent revolutionary. If we didn't use the right words when speaking about exploitation, then we'll retract them. We do not speak as extremists. We're not in agreement with those who think that the Politburo intentionally torments old Avdotya by making her wait in lines and starving her. If it were possible to spread out some enchanted red banner like a magic tablecloth in a fairy tale and say: 'Eat and enjoy yourself, Avdotya,' the Politburo would be happy to do so. Of course, the arms race is what prevents this from happening. But isn't it true that the West also has the arms race? Just the same, old women in Berlin and London don't have to put up with lines. Why is this so? The kolkhoz of the Stalin era is what oppresses old Avdotya, and the kolkhoz was Stalin's main bequest to the present leaders of the Party and government. In order to feed Avdotya, fundamental changes are necessary, changes equal to the Great Reforms of 1861, to the abolition of serfdom. Of course, this would be more difficult than sending tanks somewhere or other or launching an international crew of astronauts into space. Reforms of this sort, even in the past, were not within the power of the government alone. These days, this is even more so, no matter how great the formal power of the government. For such reforms to take place, it is absolutely essential that a vital and free society offer help to the government."

We will speak with Lucio in moderation, but you can bet that he'll get his policeman's whistle out of his pocket. Because every Party functionary, no matter what post he occupies, never ceases to be a Party watchdog.

But what am I saying? We still haven't even managed to come forward with a specific proposal. Until the great reforms take place, old Avdotya still has to live somehow. And so must the people from the industrial suburbs. And the intelligentsia. The West has many dark sides; there you get a subsidy if you're unemployed. But here where socialism is developed, why don't we institute subsidies for those who are employed? So that even they would be able to go to the Central Market sometimes and stand next to you picking over the greens from Georgia and next to Africans selecting some nice fresh meat.

But no, no. . . . Lucio has started whistling, summoning *camarada*-internationalists from the nearest police station. Gotta run, gotta run. . . . Otherwise, they'll haul me away. Old Avdotya, taking this in from the nearest line, will say to the people from the industrial suburbs, "Look, they've caught a pickpocket."

Avdotya has no political consciousness; the people from the industrial suburbs don't need freedom of speech or assembly. Old Plekhanov talked about this long ago. However, these people's need for good meat is very real, though at present an element alien in a class sense is satisfying this need at the Central Market: tribal chieftain-diplomats from African countries. Their colonial past is behind them. But what if they return to their old cannibal past?

People say that human flesh is delicious. Tastes like young pork. One progressive black gourmet has shared his thoughts. . . . Isn't it possible that the time of cannibalism passed prematurely? Perhaps it would have been better if Hitler had not been a vegetarian but a cannibal? Stalin, too, might have been satisfied if he'd eaten grilled Zinoviev with a *tkemali* sauce and enjoyed a tasty soup made from the blood of Nikolai Ivanovich Bukharin. There's *czernina,* a good Polish soup made from goose blood. Would soup from human blood be any worse? You could mix it with vinegar in exactly the same way so that it coagulates, add it to stock made from the giblets of Nikolai Ivanovich, then put in dried fruit, vegetables, a bay leaf. . . . Delicious. Comrade Stalin could breakfast on someone from the Politburo, dine on a couple of plump Central Committee members, and sup on someone from the Bureau of Investigations. He could eat up one whole staff and another would be chosen at the Party Congress. You may feel sorry for these people, but what can you do if human history requires sacrifices? The only difference is that the sacrifices used to be eaten, and now they are burned or buried. And the blacks, too, are no longer what they used to be; progress has had its effect. They buy good fresh pork, beef, lamb, and those they kill, they bury in the ground. A food product is wasted.

About blacks Avdotya once heard from Matveevna:

MAKING THE ROUNDS WITH THE SHOPPING BAG

"The first one to come to us was Paul Robeson," she said. "He at least could sing. But all these ones do is flash their teeth and dig out the bread we give them with toothpicks."

Socially irresponsible Matveevna: she didn't understand the principles of international relations. Old Avdotya is socially irresponsible too. "Oh, my oh, my. . . . Oh, how awful, how awful. What rascals they are."

And where is she now, our Avdotya? We've completely lost track of her. There she is in a mobile line. Such lines exist also. A shop helper in a blue smock wheels a cart, and in that cart are imported cardboard boxes. What's in the boxes nobody knows, but a line has formed on its own and is running after the cart. More and more people keep joining it. Old Avdotya is somewhere in the first third of this marathon line. She ought to get something. Avdotya's gray hair has become soaked, it itches under her kerchief. Her heart feels like it's entered her throat, her stomach is pressing down on her bladder, and her liver, now somewhere in back of her, aches and scratches. But you can't fall behind. If you fall behind, you'll lose the line. The helper has a hangover and is eager to breathe fresh air, so he pushes the cart without pausing. Someone in the line, exhausted, calls out: "Stop already, wait a moment. We're tired. Start selling."

A fat-assed woman from the sales staff wearing a short, dirty smock struts behind the cart. "Stop shouting or else I'm not going to start selling at all."

At that, people in the line begin to attack and intimidate their timid rebel. "If you don't like it, go home and relax." "Such a grand gentleman. Can't take a walk in the fresh air." "They know better than us where they should stop and sell. The authorities have probably told them what to do."

Following the others, Avdotya runs farther while, to spite them, the drunken helper twists and turns, now going toward a trolley car stop, now toward a bus stop. And the fat-assed saleswoman laughs. She's also under the weather. The two *oprichniks* mock the people cruelly.

In the State's present structure, types such as these possess direct and absolute power over the public—in addition to precinct policemen, apartment building managers, and others serving in an official capacity. Once, old Avdotya went to the Moscow Power Company; kind people had told her how to get there. She cried. The young women working there had not yet been corrupted, and they asked her, "Why are you crying, granny?"

"Haven't any more pages to pa-a-a-y for the electricity. They say the authorities are going to turn off the electricity. How'm I gonna live without electricity? I can't cook or wash clothes in the dark." She held out an old payment booklet, all used up, which a kind neighbor had filled out as needed.

"Oh, your payment booklet is all used up? Here's another one."

They gave her a new one, not taking a kopeck for it. Avdotya thanked them from the bottom of her heart and wished them well. You could tell how many times she must have been jeered at in various offices in her life, since she was so afraid of anyone in charge. But in this line you weren't dealing simply with people in charge; these here were the people who fed you.

Old Avdotya is running for dear life, even though black spots are appearing before her eyes. The helper keeps twisting and turning. Where he goes, the line follows, like a tail. At one sharp bend, an engineer named Fishelevich falls out of the line. His kefir bottles clink, his bones crunch. Couldn't withstand the pace. But the others do not pull out of the race, even though their strength is just about gone. Thank goodness, the helper has overdone it, made too sharp a turn, and the cardboard boxes have tumbled into the middle of the street. Several have split open. Egg whites and yolks flow out. The line is overjoyed: they'll be selling eggs. Now the mood is better. A much-needed item and you don't have to run after it anymore. The line stands still, breathing heavily and resting, while the helper and the fat-assed woman deliberate, using four-letter words. Volunteers come forward to transfer the boxes from the middle of the street to the side of the building. The selling has begun. . . .

Russians and those who have become Russified are easily appeased. Insults and difficulties are quickly forgotten, all too quickly. . . .

In view of the catastrophe, the helper and the fat-assed woman confer and reach a decision: in accordance with the request of the toiling masses, ten whole and ten cracked eggs will be sold to each customer. And instead of labeling them "Eggs for Table Use," they will be called

"Special Eggs" and given a higher price. However, in addition, plastic bags will be given out at no extra charge. OK. Old Avdotya puts the whole eggs in one plastic bag and the cracked ones, ready to scramble, in another. She pays the new price, puts everything in her shopping bag, and contentedly goes on her way. She drops into a bakery and buys some bread. Half a loaf of dark rye and a loaf of French bread. There are as yet no bread lines in Moscow. When there are lines even for bread, that will signal the beginning of a new stage in the development of socialism. With a view to the battle against cosmopolitanism, the consumption of American, Canadian, Argentinian, or any other imported grain will be forbidden. But now peaceful coexistence still prevails. The bread made from international flour tastes good. It would be good to have some meat to go with it. Couldn't get the chicken meat she wanted. Wouldn't it be nice though to get a little meat of some sort? The meat store is in front of Avdotya. The meat store's noisy, the meat store's abuzz. That means they're selling something. Old Avdotya goes in.

Not a short line, but no squabbles. Meat lines are usually among the wildest. Perhaps the smell takes us back to our primeval forebears, when representatives of various caves fought for good cuts of meat around the carcass of a mammoth. It's easier for a human being to return to a wild state than to drain a mug of beer. Everyone is familiar with certain vague urges, a certain languor in the chest. And it's not the worse thing if, in responding to such urges, one decides to douse one's mother-in-law with boiling water. But isn't it also the case that important state decisions are made by governments in this way: to suffocate people with gas, to shoot people, to let people rot in prison. But had such a citizen, such a führer-leader, been given the opportunity to climb up a tree without his pants on, perhaps the history of the nations of the world would look different.

Just these kinds of thoughts occur in a Moscow meat line when nostrils are tickled by the smell of torn flesh. Old Avdotya, our toothless predator, also catches the smell. She looks carefully. There's a nice piece lying over there. Not large and not small either. If she can only get it. Avdotya will take care of it, just like she would a small child. She will soak it twice, in cold and in lukewarm water. She will remove the outer membrane and the gristle and cut out the spongy-tissued bone for soup. From the soft part she will prepare nice little patties. Should she plead with the line for the meat in the name of Christ, the Son of God? It doesn't seem to be a mean line.

Just as she had this thought she looked around—and was nearly struck dead. Kudriashova, an old adversary of Avdotya's, was standing in line. Kudriashova, the hardened food warrior, the backbone of a large, voracious family of many children, she whom old Avdotya has on many occasions "robbed." Kudriashova had slanted shoulders and hands like hooks. Kudriashova could carry two satchels (which old Avdotya couldn't even have budged) to a distant point as long as they were loaded up with food. Kudriashova was also good at producing children. Her oldest son was already in the army and the youngest was still a toddler. A strong woman, that Kudriashova, fit for lines. She could engage a man of average build in a fist fight as an equal. However, if one had to grab—and such situations, as we know, do occur in the buying process—then old Avdotya was quicker than Kudriashova, as a sparrow is quicker than a crow. She now snatched a nice head of cabbage right out from under Kudriashova's hand and then a Tambov ham in its original packaging.

"You just wait, you old witch," Kudriashova threatened with all her might. "You wait, I'm gonna shove you."

"And I'll call a po-oliceman," replied Avdotya. "You just try shoving." But she fearfully thought to herself: "Oh no, she's gonna shove me, she's gonna shove me."

This is the right moment to explain what "shove" (*pikhnut'*) means. The old Slavic verb, *pkhati*—which is close to the present-day Ukrainian *pkhaty*—is rendered in Russian as "push" (*tolknut'*). But, *pikhnut'* and *tolknut'* are not one and the same. When the sound changes, so does the meaning. The two words exist simultaneously, not in a grammatical sense but in the way they are used. To *push* means to move something or someone aside, to distance a person. There are instances when you've pushed someone aside and you say "Excuse me" or "*Pardon*." But if you *shove*, no apology is offered, because you shove in order to smash someone to smithereens.

"Oh, she's gonna shove me," thought Avdotya. "Oh, she's gonna shove me." However, the line is quiet, not bellicose, and Kudriashova is quiet. She glances sideways at Avdotya from under her brows, but remains silent. What's the reason for this? It's not the meat, but rather the butcher.

An unusual butcher had appeared in this very store. A butcher intellectual, rather like a big-boned surgery professor of lower-class origin. He wears a neat white cap on his graying head; his face has the firm flesh of a well-nourished man. He's wearing glasses. The butcher is cheerful and cynical, just like a surgeon; not gloomy and dirty like a butcher. For him the line is an object of cheerful mockery, not an arena for high-strung squabbling. He is superior to the line. With huge but clean mitts he takes pieces of meat and places them in the showcase, on the meat tray. And in response to the grumbling of the line about slow service, he recites Pushkin's *Eugene Onegin* with abandon.

"What's that all about?" grumbles a woman with a tired face who obviously is not standing in line for the first time today. "What's that all about? You've been put here to serve customers."

"Chapter Two," the butcher answers:

> The manor where Onegin fretted
> Was so enchanting a retreat,
> No simple soul would have regretted
> Exile so pastoral and sweet:
> The hall, well sheltered from intrusion
> Of world and wind, stood in seclusion
> Upon a stream-bank; and away
> There stretched a shimmering array
> Of meads and cornfields gold-brocaded,
> And hamlets winked; across the grass
> A wandering herd would slowly pass;
> And leafy clusters densely shaded
> The park, far-rambling and unkempt,
> Where pensive dryads dwelt and dreamt.[*]

A strange picture which evokes strange ideas, and from it emerge unexpected conclusions. The first conclusion is that a butcher is bound to read Pushkin to a meat

---

[*]Alexander Pushkin, *Eugene Onegin,* trans. Walter Arndt, 2d ed. (Ann Arbor: Ardis, 1992), 37.

line. In fact, this is the main conclusion, causing one to meditate a little in the stuffiness of the store. The butcher strums in a cynical, vulgar manner on Pushkin's lyre, but nonetheless awakens fine sensations. The people are speechless, in accordance with the closing comment of Pushkin's *Boris Godunov*. They stand quietly. They don't listen to Pushkin, but they hear his poetry. Just let an important professor who is a Pushkin expert or a well-known actor recite Pushkin to a meat line. The best thing that could happen is that the people would sneer. But it might well evoke anger and hate. No, culture should be brought to the people through the authority of the state. You may say just what kind of culture would this be, just what kind of Pushkin? Let's answer this from quite an opposite point of view. And let's also answer with a question. Have you ever had an opportunity to observe how the sun rises? Not over lush subtropical greenery which is fully aware that it lives by the sun and which with scientific certainty waits for the sun to rise. And not over a quiet wooded glade covered with grass which itself appears to be a tiny fragment of the sun, which believes in the sun, and for which the sunrise is an intimate, proprietary sensation. We have in mind the sunrise over lifeless northern rocks. You might think: why does a dead thing need life? Why do the cold stones need the sun?

Covered with ice and snow, these stones lie peacefully, heavily, and monotonously in the dead of night. These stones meet the gray, short day indifferently. They receive the sharp gusts of wind on unfeeling breasts. But, over them, too, the sun rises, a weak facsimile of the hot, bountiful, or affectionate and soft sun we are acquainted with, the kind of sun that would make subtropical greenery or a wooded glade frightened and melancholy. But suddenly these rocks change. The stones turn pink, moss and lichen appear, and an uncomely insect of some sort crawls out from a crack to greet the short, festive day. Although the insect probably does not realize where the light has come from, or why the wind has abated, or why it doesn't have to be indifferent to the cold, or what this new, not really a feeling as much as a sensation of warmth and peace actually is. But were a southern or even softly temperate sun to rise over northern stones, it would be a disaster. The cold stones would crack, the lichen would dry up, the uncomely insect would perish, burn up. The cold north requires a cold sun.

You will say that this illustration is too far removed from the question we posed, too many diverse things mixed together: natural phenomena, a line in a meat store, and the public's accessibility to culture. However, there's no eclecticism here. Human souls are just as diverse as nature, but they're capable of great change. The cold sun of official culture can make these changes fruitful. But where indeed can you find enlightened butchers who know *Eugene Onegin* by heart? The finely sharpened ax rarely harmonizes with even a badly tuned lyre.

So thought the intellectual in the hat, who didn't get the kidneys, who was standing in the meat line and observing how the public gets its meat to the strumming, yes, of Pushkin's lyre. The public becomes quiet. The public grows soft.

"We are in agreement with you," says a softened someone standing in the line, "but it's meat we're after."

Behind the lenses of the professorial spectacles, in the eyes of the butcher, a mocking gleam appears, but a huge, surgically clean mitt holds the heavy meat cleaver. Old Avdotya decides to act.

"I'd like some meat," she says plaintively. "Can't stand any longer. My legs are gonna give out."

The people are tired. The people have stood for a long time and the people are disgruntled. But the enlightened butcher teaches the people by his deeds. "Which piece, grandma?" he says, deigning to manifest a monarch's favor.

"This one." And she points to the piece she had chosen.

The butcher picks up the piece of meat in his large, white mitts. It's a fine, juicy piece. And the bone would make an excellent soup. Old Avdotya can hardly believe her eyes. How lucky!

"Happy holiday to you." She wants to please the butcher so he won't change his mind.

"I'm grateful to you," the butcher answers. "But what holiday? A Party or a church one?"

The murmuring changes vein. The people are in good spirits despite the fact that the line is cramped. And with their good spirits comes understanding. "Things are hard for us," someone says, "but even more so for old people who are all alone."

Old Avdotya reaches for the meat. The butcher doesn't give it to her. Avdotya gets nervous . . . but for no reason. "If you will allow me, I'll put it in your shopping bag," says the butcher.

With the meat lying in her shopping bag, a joyous Avdotya turned to leave, and behind her the butcher said:

MAKING THE ROUNDS WITH THE SHOPPING BAG

"Thank you for your purchase."

"God bless you," replied Avdotya.

Avdotya left the store, smiling as she went. She turned the corner, took the piece of meat out of her shopping bag, fussing over it as if it were a baby and kissing it. Perhaps chicken would have been better, but chicken was not so close to Avdotya's heart. She hadn't bought any, and now she had a nice piece of meat of her very own. Old Avdotya's day had begun badly, but it was ending well. Luck was with her, so she should go looking for other opportunities. She decided to go to a store located far away, one she rarely visited. "That's OK. There'll be a bench on the way. I'll sit for a while and go on. If my luck holds out, I'll get something there. . . ."

So old Avdotya set out. She walked for a while, rested, and then went on. Suddenly, she ran into the fool. She knew his face, but she didn't know his name. This fool was no longer young; his head was scarred from burns and that's why he always wore a cap. With his sharp thin nose he would ride public transportation and make paper cutouts of people's profiles. You couldn't deny the resemblance, but you had to pay him.

The fool used to work as an artist for a firm that produced leather goods. However, once instead of inscribing the slogan "We'll Fulfill the Five-Year Plan in Four Years," he had written "We'll Fulfill the Five-Year Plan in Six Years." What had entered his head to make him do this? What's more, the blood brother of this fool—a war hero, a colonel, with military decorations, a five-room apartment, an esteemed veteran of the Great Patriotic War—

had also suddenly made a public declaration: "Today by order of the Supreme Commander-in-Chief, Comrade Stalin, snow fell." But by this time not only was Comrade Stalin no longer among the living, he was no longer even in the mausoleum. So how could he order snow to fall? People thought that perhaps the colonel was making a lame effort to be funny. They watched him closely and realized that he believed what he said—and that there was an odd gleam in his eyes. In a word, bad genes.

Perhaps this was the case. He may well be a fool, but a story is told of how the colonel's younger brother, the artist, appeared at a location somewhat removed from the part of town he lived in, where he wasn't known very well, and how he approached the very maw of a blood-thirsty, ferocious line, whose members had spent many hours in the blazing sun waiting in front of a stand where early strawberries were being sold, and he declared: "In the name of the Supreme Soviet of the USSR, I order you to sell me three kilos of strawberries." Here he displayed his right hand with the palm foremost. The palm was empty, but the public acquiesced, and he got his three kilos of strawberries. Now there's a fool for you.

The fool spotted Avdotya and said to her, "Old dearie, in Store No. 15 they are selling 'Soviet' sausage and there's no one there."

A man who was walking next to them overheard him and said, "What's this you're jabbering about? All our sausage is Soviet; we don't have Jewish sausage."

"Delicious sausage," responded the fool. "Smells good. The sort I haven't laid eyes on for a long time."

"I think he's, you know, one of those who is not all

right up here . . . ," whispered Avdotya to the man and tapped her kerchief-covered head.

"Ah," the anti-Semite understood, and went his way.

Store 15 was the very same one Avdotya was headed for. She came to a store long like a hose and dirty beyond belief. It was too dirty even for the outskirts of Moscow. You could say that it was a store begging to be satirized in the newspaper *Evening Moscow*. All the women salesclerks are dirty, crumpled, unkempt. They stand behind the counters looking as if they'd just gotten out of bed and had vodka rather than coffee for breakfast. The woman at the cash register is drunk too, and a drunk customer is standing in front of her. They are babbling about something, unable to follow each other. She speaks Russian like they do in Ryazan, he like in Yaroslavl. All the helpers have tattoos on their bony arms and on their hollow, alcohol-wasted chests. One has Stalin sitting on his chest, peeking out from under his dirty T-shirt as if from behind a curtain; another has a threatening eagle with an open beak. A third has a maritime motif: a lighthouse with the inscription "Port Arthur."

Old Avdotya knew about this store, but rarely came here. But now she has. She enters, looking around, taking in the whole picture described above and is about to leave. But then she catches sight of a sign in a far corner that says "Delicatessen." She looks there and can't believe her eyes. The fool spoke the truth. On the counter lay sausage so beautiful—Avdotya couldn't remember when she'd last seen sausage like that. Firm, like dark red marble, but you could tell just from the way the sausage looked with white marble veins of compressed fat that it must be juicy tasting. It was nothing less than a miracle! How could several crates of delicatessen-quality, wet-smoked, Party sausage turn up here, as if directly from the Kremlin's distributor? And why hadn't the people who handled this sausage made off with it themselves? Obviously, during a drinking bout, they'd put it out to be sold to the general public. There's even a label hanging there identifying the sausage as "Soviet" brand. The fool had not lied. The price is no trifle, but those other, cheap sausages are full of starch and garlic. Her friend Matveevna told her that when they made those other sausages, they mixed in the meat of water rats whose fur is used for making hats. But this meat was pure-blooded, strictly pork and beef. You could also smell Madeira in the sausage. The closer Avdotya got, the stronger the smell became. If you were to slice it thin and put it on bread, you could lunch or sup on it for a long time—you'd be on an extended holiday.

Indeed, there was a time when old Avdotya did not have to sup by herself. A samovar the color of pure gold bubbled, and there were crisp round rolls from the best bakery. He was handsome. And Avdotya had a braid the color of ripe rye. That was in '25, no, it was '23. There was a half-pound of good sausage in a package that crinkled. The sausage was called something else then, but it was the very same as this. He used to bring it and say: "Kindly consume this, Avdotya Titovna. It has Madeira in it." And he'd bring filleted sturgeon: "Kindly consume it," he'd say.

"Want d'ya want, y'ol' hag?" said the drunk, unkempt

saleswoman to Avdotya. "Gonna buy this good sausage? Only once in a decade can you get sausage like this."

But Avdotya was unable to reply. There was a lump in her throat.

"Which one will ya have?" asked the salesclerk. "This one?" And she picked up a firm, wet-smoked sausage.

But Avdotya couldn't see it. She had tears in her eyes.

"What're ya cryin' for?" asked the salesclerk. "Son-in-law chase you out of the house?"

"I don't have a son-in-law," answered Avdotya in a barely audible voice and kept sniffling.

"Must be that somebody's stolen somethin' from her," suggested the helper with the maritime motif on his chest. "They steal somethin' from you, old woman?"

"That's it," answered Avdotya through her tears.

"You do this, Mikita?" he said to the helper who had Stalin peeking out from under the curtain of his T-shirt.

By the way, this Mikita was very proud of his Stalin. In various places, in the wake of various bottles downed, he would tell the selfsame story about the sergeant who was about to be shot in '45 for raping an underage German girl. This sergeant took vengeance on the German punishing squad that had burned his house and everything in it, both living and dead. As he raped the German girl, he sobbed and cried out: "For my mother, Vasilisa Tikhonovna! For Grandpa Prokop! For my sister, Nadka! For Nadka's little boys, Lenka and Zhenka, and for Nadka's little girl, Lyudka!" At the end he forced a bottle into her at the very same place with the cry: "Death to the German occupiers!" The German girl died and the sergeant was condemned to death. They led him out to be shot and he ripped open the shirt on his chest and there was Stalin. They didn't shoot him. Sent him to a penal battalion. To be sure, Mikita would tell the story differently each time. Sometimes the sergeant was from another regiment, sometimes from a neighboring division, and sometimes Mikita himself would be that sergeant.

"You do this, Mikita?"

"I haven't even had a chance to look at her," answered Mikita. "Hemorrhoids is only thing this old woman's got worth stealing."

"I've been robbed," said Avdotya and tears poured out of her and poured out of her. She hadn't cried so much in a long time.

"If you've been robbed, go to the police. Don't get in the way of our business," said the saleswoman, and put the whole wet-smoked sausage on the scales to weigh it for the anti-Semite.

Clearly the anti-Semite had come to his senses and arrived also. He'd believed the fool. And other people were approaching the place in increasing numbers. The fool had spread the word about the "Soviet" sausage.

We need to say a word or two about the much-coveted "Soviet" sausage. Lines for sausage along with lines for oranges constitute the main combat operations in the trade war between the government and the public. You and I haven't stood in real sausage and orange lines because old Avdotya avoids them. Avdotya is crafty and the denizens of the industrial suburbs are crafty too. You rarely come across Ukrainian Makhnovites in those lines either. More often they are to be seen in the outskirts of the city where certain commodities in short supply sometimes can be found. So who stands and fights in these lines? Those from the train stations. And who are "those from the train stations?" The USSR itself. However, for oranges the USSR lines up by dint of circumstance. Instead of pears and apples, the USSR raises Kalashnikov automatic rifles in abundance, while the third world grows oranges. Here is a natural exchange beyond the realm of Marx's *Das Kapital*. The orange is not our own product, not one we are used to. The USSR gets a bitter-sour belch from it. The orange is not a serious product; it doesn't go very well with vodka. It's useful as a treat to children, but nothing more. Whereas good sausage is another matter. . . .

In Moscow's sausage stores, there is a train station mood, a train station–like stuffiness. In those sausage stores, at any moment, you expect an announcer to give you a headache as he starts squawking: "Attention. Train number so-and-so is boarding."

Trains go directly from Moscow sausage stores to the Urals, to Tashkent, to Novosibirsk, to Kishenev. Station people are not violent. The industrial suburbanite is crafty, those from the train station patient. Craftiness is rubbery, patience like iron.

It used to be that Moscow sausage stores had the pleasant smell of smoked meat. Now the smell is that of bodies long unwashed in transit. Indeed, not simply of bodies. The sausage stores are pervaded by the smell of stinking feet, feet worn out and sweaty. Not for an hour nor for two does the train station settle down, but for an entire day. Some people sit down to rest a little and take off their shoes. Iron knows how to wait. And iron has its own notions. It knows what products can be transported what distances. Hasn't education in the USSR made great strides? The percentage of educated people in the lines is high: engineers stand in them, chemists, physicists. They stand and calculate. The meat they get will make it to Gorky, as will the butter. But the meat will go bad before reaching Kazan, though boiled sausage will hold up. Beyond the Urals, you can transport smoked foods, tea, and canned goods—and those oranges for indulging children. But there is nothing better than real good smoked sausage. And iron stands and waits patiently. The USSR stands in lines for sausage. "Oh yes, my dear, to eat with a little butter and some bread, as in the old days."

Old Avdotya came to her senses. "I'm first," she cried, "I was first in line." It didn't do her any good. They shoved her away. Old Avdotya got mad. She got really mad. "People these days are bare-faced, people are all cheats nowadays." Avdotya was so outraged that she lost her temper. The kerchief went awry on her head. Pressing forward, she bruised her fist and injured her elbow. She strained with all her might and tried to shove, but at that point was shoved back herself. Some man, without even turning around, shoved her with his behind, a vanguard-quality behind, like those the members the Komsomol Youth Organization have, like reinforced concrete.

Old Avdotya regained consciousness in a hospital. Regained consciousness and right away wondered about her shopping bag. "What happened to my shopping bag?"

"What's a shopping bag to you now?" responded the nurse. "You'd better hope that your bones knit. Old bones are fragile."

However, old Avdotya did not stop lamenting her loss. "There was some choice meat in it, and some herring, three tins, and bread, and two cartons of eggs. But more than anything else, I'm sorry that I lost my precious shopping bag. Where is my provider now? Where is my bossy?"

Undergoing treatment with old Avdotya in that same hospital was Fishelevich, the engineer, a low-paid computer expert. In the hospital, as in prison, people get to know each another fast.

"Yury Solomonovich."

"Avdotya Titovna."

"What's wrong with you, Avdotya Titovna?"

"They shoved me."

"Now what sort of disease is that," said Fishelevich ironically. "I, for example, have a fractured right arm."

Avdotya looked at him intently.

"That's right," she said. "They tossed you out of the line off to the right. I remember. But don't grieve over it. Not getting eggs is much less maddening than when you don't get sausage."

Among the patients was a distinguished teacher who had fractured a hip. She took it upon herself to shame them both. "I don't understand how you can tell each other such jokes out loud."

"What do you mean jokes," said old Avdotya. "It's the

honest-to-God truth. The eggs were Bulgarian and the sausage Soviet."

"Next thing you know you'll start telling anti-Soviet stories about the Warsaw Pact," observed the teacher indignantly. She then shamed them some more, especially Fishelevich, whose Jewishness she pointed out, and promised to fulfill her civic duty.

"Excuse me," said Fishelevich, frightened by her words, "Avdotya Titovna's words are borne out in Soviet publications." And from the bedside stand he took out a large book with brown covers. Fishelevich read this book frequently. Everyone thought that it was a novel he was reading.

"Now," he said, "now here is what it says: 'Soviet-brand sausage is rightly included among the highest quality wet-smoked sausage. Its meat stuffing of grade-A lean pork and beef is larded with very small pieces of pork fat, and this creates a beautiful design when the sausage is sliced. The taste and aroma of Soviet-brand sausage is enriched by means of cognac or Madeira and a select mixture of spices. Before serving, it is recommended that the sausage be sliced into thin, semitransparent pieces.'"

"I bet that's it," said a driver with two broken legs who rolled around in a chair with castors. "Y'know, I bet that's just how important people slices it."

Here the teacher interrupted again: "This is a dissident book," she said. "Dissidents distributed this book in order to scoff at our temporary difficulties. Scoundrels, Zionists. But be aware, you tormentors, that I am an old fighter against anti-Soviet elements." And she burst into sobs out of a sense of being offended and not being able to have everyone condemned to death by a firing squad.

They gave her a sedative. But, in fact, she was right, this deputy of the regional soviet was in fact right. At the present time, when socialism has achieved full development, a culinary book about delicious and healthy food is a most dissident book, detrimental and mockingly satiric. However, Fishelevich is no fool. No, he's not.

"Excuse me," he said. "This book has been approved by the Nutrition Institute of the Academy of Medical Sciences of the USSR. The chief editor is Academician Oparin."

"Since it's been approved by an academician of the USSR," said the driver, "read on."

From then on, Fishelevich often read the book aloud. His sick companions in the hospital learned a lot of new things from it. They learned about other special kinds of sausage, about cervelat and layered sausage, and about fish soup made from sterlet, which is best when served with rich pies such as *kulebyaka* and *rasstegai*. They learned how it is good to add a piece of boiled fish to a dish of clear fish soup.

"D'you like fish, Avdotya Titovna?"

"I adore it."

"And I like meat with noodles."

No one knows who interjected this remark or even what he'd fractured. But he'd like to have meat and noodles.

"Your surname?"

"Shargomyzhsky."

"Excellent. Let's read further."

And further means an entire novella about roast beef. And an epic poem about roast turkey. And about aspic of ham à la Russe, apropos of which was stated: "the horse-radish should be served separately."

"That's correct," said the driver. "With à la Russe nowadays, the horseradish is served separately."

On account of all this reading, the teacher's temperature rose and she ceased to leave her ward. Avdotya, on the other hand, couldn't listen enough. "Oh, if only all this had found its way into my shopping bag." The shopping bag was like a blood relative to her. She dreamed about it several nights. Old Avdotya was so used to her shopping bag. How could she take another shopping bag with her to make her rounds of the lines? Old Avdotya was sad. She grieved. However, one day the nurse said to her, "Rodionova. There's a parcel for you."

Rodionova is old Avdotya's last name. Avdotya looked: it was her dear shopping bag. She looked again: it was the shopping bag. No, this wasn't happening in a dream; she was fully awake: it was the shopping bag. The choice meat was gone, naturally, and the eggs, though one of the three tins of herring was still in it. However, in return, someone put in a bottle of kefir, a little package of gingerbread cookies, and close to a kilo of apples.

Old Avdotya embraced her shopping bag, she stroked and hugged her bossy with all her heart. . . . But then suddenly she thought: now just who brought the parcel? Old Avdotya had no kith and kin. She searched in her shopping bag and on the bottom found a note written in a crude hand: "Drink, eat, granny, and get better." It was signed "Terence."

And who was this Terence? Terence was the shop helper with the maritime tattoo, the one with "Port Arthur" on his chest. So, even in the darkest of souls God's light has not been entirely extinguished. And if only for this reason, there is hope.

NINA KATERLI

THE PROFITTED
LAND

No matter what Kepker tells you, the cat's name was
Barberry, not Vasya. And all of Kepker's insinuations to
the effect that the cat would come running right away at
"Vasya," but at "Barberry" would only narrow its eyes and
twitch its whiskers, are nonsense and none of his,
Kepker's, business. Because every single being, whether
cat or person or even inanimate object, has to have the
name its owner gave it, and the owner of Barberry was
without question Nil.

As for Kepker himself, no matter how he introduces
himself, sooner or later *his* maker will summon him and
remind him who he is and what name he has. And then
out of Boris Mikhailovich our Kepker will become
Borukh Mordecaiyovich, and no subterfuges whatsoever
will help him. Let him then call someone else's cat Vasya
as much as he likes so as not to have to say "Bagbeggy"
any more than he has to.

Now even Nil, by the way, in the end turned out to
be named *Pyotr Gerasimovich Nilov 1906–1973*. The same
awaits Kepker, no matter how hard he tries to avoid it.
But as things used to be, when Pyotr Gerasimovich was
still Nil, he was also called an alcoholic or guzzler or, even

---

*The title of the original, *Zemlia bedovannaia*, is a corruption of
zemlia obetovannaia, "the Promised Land"—Trans.

more to the point, a drunkard. And if Kepker, with his characteristic sense of self-importance and impudence, said to Nil that he seemed tipsy, Nil would take offense and always correct him, that it wasn't a matter of "sogriety" but rather of his having just had a drink. And, naturally, he would remind Kepker that the skunk smells his own hole first, and that he, Citizen Kepker, better hold his tongue because everyone knows just who this person named Kepker is. But you don't worry Kepker with words like this. He's heard worse insinuations.

Pyotr Gerasimovich (then still Nil) lived in a small and puny building of red brick on a side street not far from sedate and austere Voinov Street and the puzzling and dangerous Kalyaev Street. However, whether the latter street was really dangerous or not has yet to be fully established. It's possible that it is indeed dangerous for the likes of Kepker, but that for you and me it's like mother's milk.

Nil didn't like either street—and did not think about either of them as being motherlike, though there also were some beer stands on them. He had his favorite store where they began selling not at eleven, but at ten to. We won't give the address of this store, so as not to cause good people trouble, that is, both those who run the place and those who wait outside to buy.

How little, in fact, we know about those we've lived side by side with for many years. Take Nil, for example. It's been almost three years since that grayish fall day when he became Pyotr Gerasimovich Nilov 1906–1973. With every passing year he retreats into the endless past like a parachute jumper, who, when captured by a motion-picture camera during a long jump, seems tiny in the air with arms spread out like a cross. Right in front of your eyes, the dark little cross, faceless, with outstretched arms, flies and melts away. It can only fly up—to come back down seems impossible.

And today if we try to imagine what Nil looked like, what we remember is an awkward, wide, and shortish figure, a puffy, spread-out face with a fat, round nose and eternally red cheeks, hair that stuck out in such a way that you'd have thought that someone had hacked at it clumsily for a long time with pruning shears, and small, deep-set, bearlike eyes. And just what color they were, it's already hard to recall. There's no point in believing Kepker for, although he was Nil's apartment-mate for more than twenty years, he nonetheless will lie—just out of habit. He even has the audacity to maintain that Nil resembled a Tartar, while Pyotr Gerasimovich no more resembled a Tartar than Kepker himself—and everybody knows what Kepker's looks reveal him to be. . . .

Thus Nil was small, wide, clumsy. And what else? For example, what sort of clothes did he wear? No one remembers. There was something grayish, unremarkable about them, some faded shirts, tightly buttoned at the neck, suit coats of an unintelligible color, pants without creases. Where did he get all this? Were these clothes new at one time or another? Was there a Sunday suit hanging in the wardrobe in his room? Surely there was. After all, they buried him in something that wasn't a dirty hand-me-down!

Nil worked at various jobs—as a general handyman, a stevedore, and a porter at Vitebsk Station. He even qualified for some sort of pension on which he lived during his last years. And it wasn't all that small a pension. More than enough to provide him with liquor, despite that old Kepker's hints to the contrary. Kepker himself apparently thinks that you can earn all the money in the world and then take it with you to your grave. And shouldn't he start thinking once in a while about his own end, given his advanced years?

But Pyotr Gerasimovich did not save money. He would spend all of his pension, down to the last kopeck, the first few days of the month and then exist on whatever he could borrow from Kepker. Of course, if he'd wanted to, he could have earned extra money. The neighbors on the stairwell were forever asking him to perform odd jobs: fix this faucet, or this water heater, open this lock— since the key was left inside the apartment. Nil knew how to fix faucets and open locks no better than you or I. However, for some reason, if a person wears an old suit coat, goes around unshaven, and, what's more, tipsy, people think that God himself has commanded that he be asked to fix the plumbing.

Nil never accepted money for his work. Out of principle. Consequently, no one could ever come to him complaining that water gushed out like a fountain in all directions after he'd fixed a faucet, or that the next day the lock he'd opened with the aid of an ax had to be replaced with a new one.

Kepker condemned these principles of his apartment-mate, or as he would say, tenant, and called Pyotr Gerasimovich a tramp. This no more corresponded to reality than did Nil's boorish utterances regarding

Kepker's late mother, with whom Nil was never and could not possibly ever have been acquainted since she lived and died far away in a small town called Belynichy in the Mogilev region of Byelorussia, whereas Nil spent his childhood and early youth in the Tver—now Kalinin—region and his remaining years in Leningrad. Moreover, there was no chance that he could have met Kepker's mother during the war. In the first place, he was never on the Byelorussian front, and, second, if he had been, he would not have found the old woman in her small town. In fact, he wouldn't have found the town at all. The Germans torched it in '41 and shot all the townspeople. Nil was called up only in '42.

Where Kepker was at this time is not known. He himself says, y'know, that he served in a tank battalion as a lieutenant. He even puts on medals of some sort for the Victory Day celebration on May 9, and wears them on the Imperial Parade Grounds, where he allegedly meets with his fellow soldiers. Let him do that—you may believe him as long as nobody catches him lying.

Pyotr Gerasimovich, that simple soul, believed all of Kepker's yarns. On Victory Day, he would buy a bottle with his own money and, toward evening, when Kepker returned home and entered the kitchen shouting loudly in his thin voice—"Sergeant! Glasses!"—Nil would stand at attention, just as if facing someone senior in rank, and then always fetch the glasses.

On ordinary days Kepker did not drink. He was saving up his precious health and money, which he intended to take with him to the grave.

Let's not insist that Kepker most definitely fought his

war anywhere else but in Tashkent or Alma-Ata, far removed from the battlefields. Supposedly, he even had a certificate showing that he'd been wounded in action. But everything he said about Cat Barberry was utter nonsense: that business about Nil catching it in the courtyard of another building, intending to deliver it to an agency that bought up fur-bearing animals; how he supposedly took it home only because they paid too little; and the business about the cat being named Vasya; and how Pyotr Gerasimovich didn't feed him well; and how he, Kepker, felt obliged, you know, to buy meat practically at a private market for the cat—out of pity. Nil liked the cat a lot and treated it very well. Until his last days, the cat remained his closest and dearest friend, and, as you will see later, Pyotr Gerasimovich's final thoughts were about Barberry.

The initial meeting of Nil with Cat Barberry actually occurred on a winter night. Nil woke up on his folding bed because he was cold, and he was cold because the coat that Pyotr Gerasimovich covered himself with, in place of the flannel blanket sold the day before for three rubles, didn't keep him warm at all. He hadn't closed the airing pane tightly enough, and the wind had blown it open, and now the snowflakes that were flying into the room didn't even melt right away. Pyotr Gerasimovich got out of the folding bed and, barefoot and with eyes closed, groped his way over to the window. When he touched the open frame, something outside on the street suddenly began to hiss. The apartment where Pyotr Gerasimovich lived was on the first floor, which the vainglorious Kepker called the *bel étage*. The windows of this *bel étage* were not far from the ground, in fact, lower than the average person's height. Therefore, Kepker insisted that the management nail an iron mesh to the airing panes as a precaution against thieves. Well, just beyond that mesh the freezing Nil saw, against the background of the snowstorm, a gray cat clinging to the frame of the window. He saw it and immediately broke into tears because the cat looked as though it, like Nil himself, was freezing, and the grating that separated them seemed to be that of a prison cell. They were both in prison; the cat on one side of the window and Nil on the other.

Thereupon Nil with a sob began to pull the window toward himself, ripping off the paper with which it had been sealed shut for the winter two years earlier, finally opening both sashes and letting in the cat and winter at the same time. Then the two of them lay on the folding bed under the coat, and it became considerably warmer, the cat rubbing its forehead against Nil's stomach.

The next morning, Nil named the cat Barberry, and nothing could get him to agree to another name, especially to the name Vasily. This in spite of Kepker's threats and loud protests that you can only keep pets in a communal apartment with the mutual agreement of all the tenants. In response, Pyotr Gerasimovich simply reminded Kepker that he, Kepker, was not really the tenant-in-charge, and how it was high time that he departed for the land of his ancestors. However, that same day they made up—and the cat remained Barberry. When Nil was around, Kepker called it "Kitty-Kitty-Kitty," but when he was alone with it—Vasya.

With the appearance of Barberry, Nil had new concerns to occupy himself with. He even made a paper lamp shade for his light and, when summer came, he made a habit of going fishing. He used to like to rest near the Peter and Paul Fortress. There on the bank of the Kronwerk Canal, directly opposite the zoo, is a meadow where people walk their dogs. There are old poplars growing in this meadow and in the shade under them on grass soft like in the country, you can lie and listen to the noises of invisible animals coming from the other bank. One growls, another even grunts, undoubtedly a hippopotamus, something Nil had never seen in his whole life. For although he had lived in Leningrad for nearly half a century, for some reason or another he'd never been to the zoo.

Nil would bring with him to the bank a "wee bottle" in the pocket of his suit coat. He'd drink in a leisurely manner on the grass and lie there as long as he wanted, gazing up into the sky and listening to the sounds from the other side of the river. Then he'd get up and go talk with the dog owners. The latter were proud people, but Nil knew well how to talk to them.

"I used to have one just like yours," he would begin gingerly, approaching a dog. "He was called Rex. Also a wolfhound, except that he had a hooklike tail. A prizewinner!"

"That's a Doberman pinscher," the dog's owner would say, unbending somewhat. "You shouldn't pet it. It might bite."

But dogs never bit Nil.

Now that he had his own cat, Nil stopped making advances to strangers' dogs. After drinking his "wee bottle" and dozing off for forty minutes or so, he would walk across the small bridge to the embankment, find a good place on the parapet, take out a can of worms, stick a worm on a hook, and skillfully cast his line. He didn't attempt to cast far out, where undoubtedly there were large fish, for ruff and small perch were best caught near the bank among the moving green water plants and bright candy wrappers.

Nil was a lucky fisherman. Fish bit for him any time of the day, during any kind of weather, despite all the rules. As everyone knows, you don't catch fish just before it rains, or at noon when it's hot. Yet he would manage to fill up a whole plastic bag with various small fry, board a bus, and head home where a hungry Barberry was waiting for him.

"Sixty years old and has no more sense than that of a child," Kepker would say every time he caught sight of Nil with his plastic bag. "It'd be better if he'd find something useful to do!"

Just *what* in his opinion Nil should do, Kepker never explained. And Nil didn't ask. He never asked. And what it was that Kepker occupied himself with remains a mystery, even now. Maybe it would be a good idea to find out what that really was.

Once in a while, suddenly, a small leaf that has turned yellow comes off a tree prematurely and, quivering in the breeze, slowly begins to fall. What has caused it to wither and fall in June? Perhaps some disease—who knows—but, looking at it, all you do is think: it's summertime now and hot; oh, how long it will be before fall comes; all the leaves on the tree are still healthy, green. But then, before you've had a chance to say "Jack

Robinson," they've turned yellow and are falling down one on top of another. Not a single leaf remains on the tree; they all fall to the ground.

This is what Nil thought too every year when he noticed the first yellow leaf eddying to the ground. Now there were already more than enough of these leaves. Whole schools of them were swimming in the puddles, flat and not yet dried out and curled up, and the puddles were still bright as in summer, the blue summer sky reflecting in them.

Nil walked along the street, leaving the unloved Voinov and Kalyaev Streets behind him. At this early hour of the day he was very sober and quiet. Last night, when he made up his mind to go *there,* he denied himself his usual drink, and today he'd shaved. For some reason he'd put on his winter hat—couldn't find any other—and then started out. . . .

He had an uncommon desire to eat something. Since he usually craved a drink in the morning, there was a strange sensation in his head: a "booming" hollowness, like that of a tall, empty building.

Nil would seldom look around as he walked down the street. When he trotted up to a store, feeling in his pocket for rubles and going through his small change with a clammy hand, he was always businesslike and preoccupied. He would figure out what he had enough for: a full-sized bottle, a "wee" one, cheap red wine, or, as was sometimes the case, only beer. As far as people were concerned, he would notice only how many there were in the line in front of the store's doors, and if someone he knew was standing in it.

Today, on his walk, he was all eyes. He met respectable people, dressed like Kepker on his days off. They were walking in the opposite direction and carrying large briefcases. Nil was sure they all must be directors. They were so clean, proud, like the dog owners. And many of them, women in particular, were holding the hands of small children. Nil then recalled that in his whole life (wasn't it funny) he'd never even once walked along a street holding the hand of a child. He thought about this a little, and it wasn't that he felt sorry for himself, but he somehow marveled at the fact that an old man like himself, who had lived so long, imagine, had never had to carry a briefcase, never had any children of his own.

To be sure, this was also the case with Kepker. No relatives whatsoever. But with Kepker it was different, since he belonged to the people who came from nowhere and belong nowhere.

And he began to look around more attentively, at houses with beautiful balconies, at a shiny foreign car, at a sleepy Gypsy woman who had been selling flowers since early morning.

Although Nil had been a city dweller almost his whole life, for some reason he was used to thinking of himself as a country being; regularly, he would argue with Kepker about what was more important, the city or the country. And he would always say that it had to be the country because it feeds everyone.

Kepker would then begin to babble about technology and industry. But who's going to listen to this nonsense of his. It isn't Kepkers who till the soil. And they aren't the ones who become deformed from working at factory benches.

However, today the morning was special with those blue puddles with the leaves floating in them. Today even the buildings were special, elegant, and Nil felt that he loved this city, and for some reason pitied it, and all its people, even the important ones with the briefcases. And he felt sorry, too, for Kepker, who because of his origins didn't have the right to look as a natural owner would on puddles and trees and rejoice; they were alien to him, the poor devil. Nil was also preoccupied with the certainty that he would soon die. This was not frightening, but, on the contrary, somehow comforting, like something that obviously had to happen. His time was coming. And this premonition made him feel even more pity for everything around him, as if without him all these streets and these houses with balconies would not be looked after and would vanish.

Nil walked faster and faster. He crossed a streetcar line, passed through a quiet alley so narrow that you felt like walking sideways, and at the corner suddenly stopped. He'd walked all the way from his building without a thought about how he would approach this place, how he would enter its door, and what all this was really for. He simply had walked there and that was it. Now that he had reached the place, he grew timid and couldn't move a step. He stood a while and then a while longer, looked across the street at the green domes, the crosses of gold, pulled off his cap, and smoothed his hair with his fingers. He felt like crossing himself. He even raised his hand to his forehead. But then, for some reason, he again became timid and little by little sidled back into the alley, as if behind him somewhere in one of the doorways Kepker might well be smirking at him maliciously.

If you think that after this splendid morning Nil gave up drink and gave himself over to reflection, you're sadly mistaken. He drank as before, perhaps even more, and he and Kepker abused each other as before, but that special pity for houses and streets which had come over him was now extended to an even greater degree to his cat Barberry. He kept thinking about what would happen to the animal when they buried him, Nil, in the earth. He tried to get Kepker to talk about this, but that one would never come up with anything more intelligent than waving his hands and shouting, "He's jabbering! Doesn't know himself what he's jabbering about! Just look at him, he's getting ready to die! You shouldn't drink so much, that's what I say!"

Kepker didn't understand a thing. And this made Nil spit on the floor and use the "mother" words, as if referring to Kepker's old lady, the one who had passed away in the little town of Belynichy.

Of course, this is a sentimental story. But the reader is not obliged in any way to wail tearfully, "Oh, what a pity, what a pity." Two lonely, neglected old men living out their days in a worthless, good-for-nothing building—in all probability with none of the conveniences. Why, those poor, unfortunate, good-natured old men!

Nothing about them evokes pity; there's nothing about them to be appreciated. As for the worthless, good-for-nothing building, well, if the apartment in which our heroes lived had been condemned as uninhabitable, they would have been put on a waiting list long ago—and since that's never happened, their living conditions can't be so bad after all.

But what's even more important, as you can see for yourself, is that one is an alcoholic, riffraff, who lolls on a cot with absolutely no bedding, hugging a dirty cat, and the other is no one knows what, maybe even an underground speculator in foreign currency, with a revolting accent and eternal dandruff about his shoulders. What is there really to feel sorry for!

And if you take it into your head to be moved by their friendship—"Ah, though the old men squabble occasionally over trifles, they've nonetheless lived next to one another in virtual harmony for twenty years"—then you've been duped again.

Just what sort of "harmony" has there been? Please let me give you an example: in the fall, when the weather was already pretty nasty, Kepker, returning in the evening from work, discovered Nil sleeping near the front door. And what do you think he did? Did he help him up? Take him indoors? Or at least try to rouse him? You don't know Kepker! He went into the apartment very quietly, heated up some dinner for himself, and, having eaten, sat down in front of the television set to watch *Seventeen Moments of Spring*. Only then did it occur to him to take out the garbage. He prized himself out of his chair, went to the kitchen and got the slop bucket, which was almost full, and went outside.

Nil he found in the same place, next to the stoop. He was not asleep now, but sitting, leaning back against the wall and staring up at the evening sky, which was timidly emerging from beyond the roof of the high building on the opposite side of the street. Kepker, pursing his lips, walked past, not even so much as glancing at Nil, and turned and went under the arch into the courtyard, made a clatter with the bucket, and came back all at the same unhurried pace.

"Y'know what?" Nil shouted to him from the ground. "I just had a dream."

Kepker said not a word, but pursed his lips still more, so that the corners of his mouth turned down. Nonetheless, he stopped, looked down at Nil in an ironic way, and even raised one eyebrow.

Then, holding on to the wall, Nil raised himself and, looking around cautiously, whispered in Kepker's ear that he had just seen Trotsky himself in a dream.

"Just like in real life," whispered Nil, agitated and reeking of vodka. "He was making a speech, trembling all over like the plague, and right here"—Nil stuck his finger straight into the lips of the dumbfounded Kepker—"right here there was actually drool!"

Indian summer had come to an end, everything around had grown dark, the trees were bare, and at night outside the window of Nil's room a nagging rain pounded and pounded. Nil did not have a moment's peace. It was as if he, too, were being tormented by insomnia. He couldn't close his eyes until the very break of dawn, when the window turned from gray to white and it became obvious how dirty the window was, all streaked from the rain.

Nil stopped trying to talk with his apartment-mate

about death. Kepker didn't understand anything and was afraid, as well he should be, for weren't the people of his nation destined after dying to burn in eternal flames?

In the morning, lying with the cat on his folding bed, Nil grinned when he heard Kepker's mincing steps, the noise of water running, and the clinking of the tea kettle in the kitchen. The greedy Kepker was not lazy about getting up at the crack of dawn and dragging himself in the rain through the whole city to earn money that he did not even know how to spend well on himself. And just once did it suddenly occur to Nil: what if Kepker were running to work not for the money but to escape death? That's what he was doing. He ran and ran, passing death by, thinking that by keeping busy he could outwit it. "Why take this one," Death might say. "He's busy. Nil is another matter. He has time for everything, and for death even more so." But again Nil was not a bit terrified. Why should he be? He was a working man, a simple soul; he fought at the front during the war. It is unlikely that after death he would be passed over and treated badly. He just didn't think this would happen. He simply wasn't afraid; that was all. With a certain sense of relief, he thought about the ragged overcoat with which he and Barberry used to cover themselves, and about how, if he, Nil, remained among the living, he would have to wear that coat all winter long, and about how he would not need it if he died before winter.

But then there was the cat to think about. . . .

One day at the end of October, the rain took a break and the sun shone for an entire day. The sky, although cold, was blue; in the early morning the temperature had dropped down low and under your feet the puddles crunched. Nil went out holding his cat Barberry next to his chest under his suit coat. The cat was sleeping. It was fast asleep when Nil got up from his folding bed, and even now hadn't woken up, and, heavy and warm, it was breathing deeply under the suit coat.

"Sleep tight, you pest," said Nil to the cat so as not to yield to feelings of compassion.

The cafeteria he'd found and designated long before. It had low windows, its airing panes were never shut, and out of it a delicious steam wafted onto the street. The cafeteria was always clean. On the tables were flowers in earthenware vases and at the checkout on a stool sat a fattish women in a white cap. The woman's face seemed sad but not evil, and Nil, looking at her, believed that she was a person who wouldn't offend anyone.

Now he approached the cafeteria and, stopping in front of one of the airing panes, glanced inside. He saw the woman towering in her usual place. She was yawning. Nil then pulled out the sleeping cat that had been nestled to his chest, stood on his tiptoes, and shoved Barberry in through the airing pane. The cat was not at all surprised nor frightened to find itself behind glass on the inside windowsill, and it began to stretch. Quickly, Nil turned his back to the window and ran away, hobbling in his haste. That day he got so drunk that he didn't turn up at home until the next morning, having come to in a "sobering up" station. Returning home in a foul mood, he met Kepker at the doorstep to the apartment.

"Here he comes, the drunken *khazer!*"* yelled Kepker. "And I have to go looking for him at police stations all over the place!"

Just who this *khazer* was, Nil, naturally, did not know. Most likely some scum or other, but he didn't feel like answering back. He simply didn't have the strength. He felt weak and down, as if he hadn't spent the night in a sobering-up station, but on a cement sidewalk. So he told Kepker to pack up and go home to the Profitted Land where smarties of his kind are waiting impatiently for him, and not to bother the working man to whom this country really belongs.

Nil said all this to Kepker somewhat limply, without any real satisfaction. And likewise Kepker didn't begin to shout back about the Profitted Land, because he had no time: he was rushing off to work—to outwit his own death.

For Nil death came one night in November, just before the holidays commemorating the October Revolution. Since evening, flags, darkened by water, had flapped wet in the rain. Important statesmen looked sternly down from the walls of a huge building on Liteyny Prospect. Kepker, grumbling, was washing the gas burners in the kitchen. Nil had drunk next to nothing—one bottle of rotgut. He was saving a half-liter bottle for the next day; they wouldn't sell you anything then, those scoundrels. He finished the bottle and immediately fell asleep, and in the morning he was gone.

---

*Yiddish for "pig."

It was Kepker who arranged the funeral. He went around to each of the apartments in the building carrying with him a piece of paper on which he recorded everyone's name, and each time he repeated the very same phrase: "Please, do as much you can to take part in the burial of Comrade Nilov. As much as you can afford."

Some gave twenty kopecks, some thirty, some as much as a ruble. The money Kepker collected was, frankly, too little, but perhaps the building's management helped or maybe Kepker forked out money of his own, but the result was a decent funeral. There was even a wreath with a ribbon on it, from the old women of the house committee, the very same ones who just a year before had gone to the police with a petition to resettle Nil as an alcoholic to a special suburb out a hundred and one kilometers on the commuter line. On the ribbon in gold letters was written: "To Pyotr Gerasimovich Nilov, from a Group of Comrades."

So then, from that day on, Nil became *Pyotr Gerasimovich Nilov, 1906–1973,* and so he will remain for quite some time, until that day when the bulldozer at the cemetery scoops up his grave as one no longer attended to. However, this will not happen for a while, that is, until after Kepker's death—and it looks like he'll live a long time.

And what will become of them both when even the little mound with the epitaph "Borukh Mordecaiyovich Kepker" also disappears? What names will they be given in the hereafter? Does one need a name there at all? How will they meet one another there? Will they recognize each other when both their bodies have turned to dust, one and the same dust for both Nil and Kepker, in their common, "Profitted Land?"

These are the kind of odd questions that sometimes come to mind, but there is no need to seek answers. Let the dried-up leaves fall from some unknown affliction under our feet on a bright summer day. There is absolutely no reason to perceive this normal event in nature as some sort of bad, mystical sign. Also, one should not believe idle rumors. Rumors are floated among us not for evil purposes, but rather to while away the time, from boredom, so that there is something to talk about when you sit by the gate in the evening. It's really foolish to listen to old women, even if they happen to be members of the house committee. Old women have watery brains and weak eyes. Out of fear, they always see a sober man as a drunk. Thus, all conversations to the effect that Kepker took up drinking are nonsense, fiction. In the first place, it is well known that as a people *they* do not drink. Then, too, how could he possibly drink, worrying so much as he does about his health and being frightened to death that he may be asked to retire?

There was even a funeral dinner, and traditional Orthodox memorials were held on the tenth and fortieth days after Nil's demise. Everything was carried out according to custom. Kepker did a really fine job of organizing everything. This despite the fact that these are not the customs that *they themselves* observe. Only a fool refuses to drink at a funeral dinner, or a swine who has no respect for the deceased. Boris Mikhailovich also drank with the tenants. He drank and conducted himself with utter decorum: he didn't sing, dance, or fight. As for his supposed weeping, you can rest assured that this is utter nonsense. Whatever was there for him to cry about? Should he feel sorry for a drunkard who shared a communal apartment with him for twenty years and never once washed the common areas they both used? An alcoholic, who was forever pestering people to lend him some money? No, Nil always paid back money conscientiously, on time, so you can't say a bad word about him in this regard. But really, does this give one reason to cry at his funeral feast?

Most amusing, though, was the fact that in the winter Cat Barberry returned. Kepker was coming back from the bread store one day, and on the landing he stumbled over something soft. The cat let out a screech. Kepker cursed, but then looked closer in the darkness and recognized Nil's pet. Kepker wasn't overjoyed, but he let the cat into the apartment and even poured it some milk, yesterday's to be sure.

It would be nice to be able to write that after Nil's death Kepker became a sensitive and kind old man who took pleasure in keeping the orphaned cat in memory of his late apartment-mate and friend. But, alas, this would be a lie. The cat is indeed living for the time being with Kepker, and has lived there three years already. From the street you can see him, fat as a pillow, lying on the windowsill next to the pot with the crooked cactus, dozing. But every time Kepker brings home fish in his string bag and the old women who are always sitting on the bench next to his building maliciously ask him—"For the kitty?"—he answers them didactically, "I do not like animals. I will not hurt them nor let them starf, but still, I don't see why one has to like them. An animal is nothing more than an animal, even when it's Bagbeggy. Now a human being—has to be treated like a human being."

Such a pain, that Kepker!

And there are also rumors that under the new Five-Year Plan, the building where they live is going to be torn down. The tenants will all be moved to newly built sections of the city. Those who are eligible for separate apartments will receive them. But the building will be pulled down right to the foundation. Then in its place a new building will be erected, a spacious building of glass and cement, and to this building will come new owners, serious, severe people with briefcases, much more suitable for life and work in that serious district near Voinov and Kalyaev Streets.

And the ground next to the sinking wall of the present building, where burdock and dandelions and other weeds now grow, will be plowed over, spaded, and planted with tulip bulbs. But it also may happen that no open ground will be left at all, that it will all be taken up by the cement building, right up to the sidewalk. However, why make wild guesses and listen to old women's gossip!? Whatever will be, will be.

VASILY BELOV

THAT KIND
OF WAR

Vanya, Darya Rumyantseva's son, was killed at the front in
'42, but the official notification didn't come until the
spring of '43. The notification, with its official stamp and
unreadable and consequently quite suspicious signature,
took more than a year to reach Darya. Because the notification was so long in coming, and even more important,
because the signature on it was unreadable (nothing more
than a hook with a little loop), Darya decided that the
notice was fake, something concocted by an evil person.

Any time gypsies were passing through the village,
Darya went to see them and paid them to tell her Vanya's
fortune. And every time it turned out that the official
notification was a fake. The cards were always favorable.
To her, Darya, the seven spot was always dealt, and next
to the king of hearts would turn up either the ace of dia-
monds—signifying an official building—or the six of
clubs. The king with the six could only signify a trip for
Ivan: sometimes it was a trip to an official building, at
other times a trip away from it. To be sure, the king of
spades was around all the time, that black Antichrist
with a sharp sword in his unclean hand. Nothing could
be done about it. Ivan had left home not to have a good

time but to go to war. But then again neither the ten of spades (signifying a sickbed) turned up next to Ivan's card even once nor the ace of spades, which stands for a mortal blow.

The cards that turned up were cheerful, almost all reds. Darya would come back from the fortune-teller joyous, in bright spirits, and she wouldn't regret that she'd paid with the soured goat's cream or the last of her precious prewar Chinese tea. She'd feel at peace, and she'd visit every house in the village just to repeat over and over: "My Vanya's alive, he's alive. The notification means nothing; it's a fake."

And all the people, especially the womenfolk, were sincere in their boisterous confirmations of Darya's thoughts. Darya, coming home afterward, would start the samovar, and for a long time would sip hot boiled water with dried turnip in place of sugar and feel a sense of comfort. On the table, the samovar would sing out merrily; cheerful noises came streaming out of it. Beneath the white pine floor an unsuspecting mouse would rustle gently. The clock on the wall ticked as before, when her son Ivan was here. And Darya would wait patiently for the end of the war.

During the evenings, fall and winter, she would hang the lock that didn't work and was as old as the copper samovar onto the hasp of the gate, push a small birch stick into the loop, and then go to the stable to guard the horses.

In the heated guard's cubicle the stove crackled as it burned, and there was the smell of horse flesh and steam from the sweaty, felt horse collars. Harnesses hung in rows on wooden pegs. Darya counted them out loud, lit the lantern, and made the rounds of the stable.

The long dry passageway with two rows of stalls was clean and inviting. The horses were peacefully munching hay. The munching merged into a single even, endless sound, like that of a warm, gentle rain with the sun shining. Darya loved to listen to the horses eating. As she walked down the long passageway, a feeling of peace and contentment would come over her. She didn't realize that what she delighted in was nothing more than the peacefulness of horses exhausted and now at day's end satisfying their hunger. Not greedily, but in an unhurried, peasantlike fashion, the horses were picking out the stalks of the fodder with their soft lips. They greeted the light of the lantern with deep snorts as it passed them by. Darya would pass through the stable from one end to the other and, feeling satisfied with herself, would drowse all night in the heated cubicle thinking about her son, Ivan.

At daybreak she would return home, dragging with her a broken piece of wood, a peg left behind, or a rotting board. Getting firewood exhausted Darya and was especially tiresome in the wintertime. In the summer she lit a fire indoors only every other day to save a little on wood and even took to boiling potatoes in the samovar. It was simpler and cheaper to do it that way. The potatoes, the smaller ones at least, cooked quite quickly; the hot water which she then drank in place of tea also seemed somehow tastier.

The first two years of the war Darya kept her own

goat. "I didn't have any farm animals, and this ain't no farm animal either," Darya would say as she drove the goat out of other peoples' vegetable gardens.

The goat was an utter tramp. It was forever climbing up some way onto the roof, bleating and running along the edge, not knowing how to climb back down. And Darya, alarmed, would have to call on old man Misha for help. Then it would get into the kolkhoz rye field and, when that happened, Darya, just like everyone else, was fined five to ten days of work. In actual fact, Darya couldn't drink the milk from the goat. It stank to high heaven; it didn't smell real. On account of all this, Darya gave her "cow" various nicknames: "Valka," "Tiny Pinch," but never with any malice, for she generally felt sorry for animals.

One time early in the spring, quite to Darya's surprise, the goat got herself pregnant and then, even though she was fed no more than what could be found round about, brought forth two fluffy and large-foreheaded kids. Darya soon traded one kid, a female, to her neighbor Surgan for three pounds of sheep's wool, to be made into felt for boots. The other, a billy, grew without anyone noticing, and turned into a lustful blockhead with a big brow. He would even leap on people, snorting, making a shameless grimace with his lips, and wiggling his tail. The beard he had was not so much a beard as a tangled ball of burdock burrs. His horns were constantly bloodied because the children had trained him to butt. So Darya didn't get very upset when she lost her billy, though it was too bad that this happened before she could deliver the goat to satisfy part of her meat requisition. If she'd done this at the right time, she wouldn't have those unfulfilled obligations now.

Darya was still of working age. She had to satisfy the whole tax, which meant delivering eggs, meat, wool, and potatoes. She delivered all this, having to buy some things or substituting one item for another to do so; it was only in "meat" that she came up short. Actually, her monetary payment was still entirely unremitted, not to mention her payments for insurance, the State War Loan, and the additional, voluntary tax. She hadn't even made these payments for the previous year, 1942, and Pavel Neustupov, known as Kuverik or The Gimp, who was the same age as her Vanya but who had not been drafted into the army for health reasons, had brought Darya statements of what she owed for the new year back in January. At the time, Darya carefully put the green and pink slips of paper in the little box where she used to keep tea, while Pavel fastened his case with its official papers and began to lecture Darya, "When's it goin' to be, Comrade Rumyantseva? Let's not quarrel. Gotta settle with the government. You gotta."

"I know I gotta, Pasha," Darya said. "How could I even think, my friend, that you don't have to settle? I know you have to." And she began to get the samovar out, genuinely happy to have a guest.

Before the war Pavel and Vanya went on sprees together. They even stayed with one another, and Darya regarded Pavel as a member of her own family. She wanted to give him some sort of treat, to chat a little with him. But The Gimp left for another household, and Darya watched him go, recalling once again her own son Ivan.

And then in the winter, when her billy goat was fully grown, Darya wanted to turn him in to satisfy the meat requisition, but she didn't succeed in doing so.

Here's what happened. One day the farm director rode into the village and put his gelding in an empty stall in the stable. Darya wanted to remove the saddle and bridle from the gelding, but the director, who was drunk, told her not to touch anything, since he would be riding back to his office before long. Darya went home, for in the daytime there was nothing to guard in the stable. Besides, this gelding wasn't from their stable. The gelding ate hay and, since it was bridled, bit its tongue, hurt itself badly, and had to be slaughtered. The kolkhoz board ruled that not only was the director guilty, but Darya as well.

The director paid his fine in cash. He sold something and paid. Darya, on the other hand, had no money. Everyone knew this, and in the minutes of the board meeting the following decision was recorded: "In view of the careless damage done to the kolkhoz's gelding, a privately held goat is to be taken from the household of guardswoman Rumyantseva."

Hunger had somehow imperceptibly taken hold, gnawing its way little by little into the country. Certainly, this is why no one threw up their hands when the first old woman on the kolkhoz died of starvation. No one was surprised, either, by the fact that the doors of the villagers' homes were now almost never shut due to the great number of beggars.

Along the roads walked more and more old men of varying appearance from places far away carrying short sticks and sacks. Pitifully poor, worn-out old women and cripples with baskets dragged themselves along. Adolescents came carrying canvas bags sewn for school use. Children drifted from village to village, from house to house. Children of all sorts—starting with those who had barely learned to walk and extending to those a little older. The women of the village would ask them, "Are you a boy or a girl?" Because from their dress it was hard to guess which—and no matter what, women need to know about everything.

The children begged for alms, using expressions they had learned by heart, "Please, for the fire victims," or they would say they were orphans. They would stand by the doors, indifferent, not raising their eyes. People would give them something, but when people had nothing to give, they'd turn around just as indifferently and head for someplace farther on. Now the old men, they'd be quick with their supplication at the doorstep, so that a hut wouldn't lose its heat. Facing the corner where the icons were placed, they'd cross themselves and say, "Lord, grace this house with abundance and tranquillity, preserve it from fire and pestilence, and protect its owner against sword and bullet and evil men. Give as much as you can, for the sake of Christ." In response, the old women would whisper prayers, meekly, fervently. . . .

The beggars would make their sleeping arrangements while it was still light, so as not to get lost in the darkness, and rare was the home that refused them shelter. The local women would sit them down at the table, divvy up the soup, ask them whose people they were and what their names were, if they had any family and did they have a home, and what news there was from far away places. The beggars would warm themselves on ancient stove benches. Those who were good at telling fairy tales would gather round a group of listeners.

In the peasant hut the birch splinter burned virtually without smoke, the wind howled beyond the windows, and magical fall nights were made shorter by merry and awe-inspiring events in a world of hard knocks.

"And didn't ya hear, my dear, what happened that summer over there in Dikovo?" a beggar woman would begin in a quiet, soothing way, addressing her hostess— and everyone would grow silent.

"No, grandma, I didn't hear. What was it?"

First the old woman would blow her nose thoroughly into an old rag of some sort, fold her hands, dried out and shiny from age, and shake her head as if to convey reproach. "Doesn't everyone know what happened in Dikovo?"

The hostess would sit by the fire, and the children would poke each other in the ribs and huddle closer.

"Well, my dear, in the village of Dikovo lived a family. A man, his woman, and two kiddies. When war spread o'er the land, that man, of course was drafted right away. Now his woman saw him off, and then was left alone with the children. The woman, big-boned and portly, was called Maryuta. Well, they lived this way a year, and then another. Suddenly people there overheard in the cellar at Maryuta's place either a small dog or pig whining at night. So, when evening approached, my dears, a whining and also a sobbing began. . . ."

"In her cellar?"

"In her cellar, my dear. And then people began noticing that Maryuta's belly had become bigger. Why did she have such a belly if her husband was away at war? Wouldn't it seem that she'd done something sinful to make this happen?"

While spinning her tale, without thinking about it, the storyteller would make tiny crosses over her narrow, small chest, the hostess would express amazement and clap her hands, and the children would listen fearfully to the story about the devil.

From the beggar woman's story, they found out that this Maryuta would lock the devil in her cellar during the day, and in the evening he would squeal and beg to be released. At night she would let him out, and one day she gave birth to a child. And supposedly, when the child was being washed in the bathhouse, one of the old women present noticed that it had a very short little tail, no bigger than a thimble. When the people got together and cleansed the entire house with heather smoke, they saw nothing at all—but there were hoof tracks in the snow leading from the cellar.

In her simplemindedness, the old woman didn't even notice that the story was supposed to have taken place in the summer, at the height of the haying season. Her listeners didn't pay attention to the fact that there was snow in summer either.

In the morning, the beggars rose early together with their women hosts. They left for God knows where. They moved on and others came to take their place. And so they came, wave after wave, and there seemed to be no end in sight to this gloomy period of hunger.

Soon there was absolutely nothing to eat. The small supply of grain stored before the war had long since been consumed. The women had scraped clean the grain bins and cribs with thin grouses' wings. In those homes where cows had been butchered and eaten, the potato came to the rescue. To supplement their supplies, the women would go to a distant kolkhoz where grain was still available, and barter goods for it. Out of trunks came festive headscarves reminiscent of the old time, kerchiefs, men's suit coats, boots. They would pile all these items on a sled and, after a good cry, go off in businesslike fashion in pursuit of a bitter bargain. Ten pounds of grain in exchange for a pair of new calfskin boots, half a pood of potatoes for an elaborate lace headscarf. Holding back their tears, the women did not try to haggle. They drove back, bringing home a small amount of grain and a few potatoes— so few you could count them one by one. Their burden was light, so light the sleds didn't crunch down the snow. And oh, how quickly did the large prewar trunks, not very full even before such trips, empty out.

To be sure, even under these circumstances there were situations that made the women laugh. Like the time one woman, merry in spite of her despair, exchanged a colorful cashmere shawl acquired before she was married for two pots of curdled milk. "To hell with it! At least this time I'll have my fill!" Another transported a bottle of cabbage soup twenty versts in freezing weather. A third bought a lame chicken for a bundle of brittle, brand-new war bonds. As the saying goes: you laugh and cry from the same mouth.

Darya had Ivan's good wool-blend suit. Ivan had

bought it three weeks before the war began. He hadn't even had time to enjoy it when the dreaded messengers galloped up on their horses, accordions began to play, and women and girls all around began to wail.

At times when life seemed unbearable to Darya, when her heart ached badly, she would fetch the suit from the storeroom, caress it, and take in Vanya's scent, distant and now permeated with the mustiness of the chest.

Once she noticed that there was a loose button on one of the sleeves. Another time she turned the pockets inside out and found a kopeck and shreds of coarse tobacco. Ivan had taken up smoking earlier while doing his required stint in the military. For many hours Darya would sit by herself, agitated, shedding assuaging tears. She hid the kopeck in the sugar bowl. Working slowly in order to extend her happiness, she sewed the button onto the sleeve. But she was unable to pluck up her courage and go with the women to barter it, even when her legs began to swell.

On May Day, her neighbor, Misha, the gray-haired old man who blurted things out, bought the nanny goat from her. Half of the purchase price Darya took in pota-toes, the other half in cash. The cash, seventy-five rubles to be exact, Darya handed over to the tax collector that very day. The potatoes she divided: one basket for eating and another basket to use for seeding. So that she, like all good people, would be able to plant at least one small patch. But, in order not to die of hunger, she soon had to boil the seed potatoes in the samovar as well. When peo-ple began to till their vegetable gardens, Darya felt really sorry. Somehow she should plant at least one small patch, or even half a patch. Finally, she made her decision to go with the women and barter.

In exchange for Ivan's suit, Darya received half a sack of potatoes. The cuttings she used to plant one and a half patches. She lived on the leftovers of the cuttings and on little flat cakes made from clover flowers almost until the Feast of the Kazan Virgin in mid-July.

A pleasant warm summer came to the village. Every day Darya went with the women to mow the hay. The time passed more quickly when she was part of this group. She wanted to eat less, and her anguish seemed to diminish. When they stopped to rest, Darya sat next to the other women and warmed her swollen legs in the sun. She kept feeling like dozing off. She rarely joined in the conversation, and at times didn't notice her mosquito bites.

"You should go home, Darya dear, and lie down for a while," they'd say to her. She'd shake herself and, ashamed of her weakness, would say affectionately and tenderly, "My poor ol' head is going 'round, girls. It really goes 'round 'n' 'round. It really does."

Clouds kept passing over them. In the hot grass the crickets sang tirelessly. Their sound blended with an unceasing, faint ringing in her ears, like the ringing you get when you've inhaled carbon monoxide.

Drowsily, Darya again bent her head, smiling when the wind caressed her furled brow. She would get onto her feet with difficulty and take hold of the rake.

Starting to work again, it seemed to her as if she were just about to fall. However, little by little new strength somehow came to her; it even amazed Darya. She wouldn't leave for home until all the others had. On the way she, like the others, picked juicy sweet stalks of angelica growing under the bushes. Stripping away the rough outer peel, she ate the crunchy pulp. And she gathered sorrel, which was beginning to wither.

The sun would expand, turn red, and go down behind the horizon. The cows would come back from grazing. By the stream the corncrake would try its voice, as if there were no war anywhere.

At home Darya would feel better. She would get the samovar going and put three or four potato cuttings in it. Her samovar came to a boil very fast. She would not even carry it to the table, but leave it by the stove grate and, while she ate the potato, look it all over and talk to it, "Now bubble a little more for me, now bubble some more. See how he talks."

Darya had chatted in the very same way to the goat, and she also had talked to the mouse who lived under the floor. But long ago the goat had been bought and butchered by neighbor Misha, and the mouse no longer lived under the floor, so now Darya talked to the samovar. "All right, all right. I'll show you! I'll just put the cover on your chimney, and then you'll stop."

The samovar would calm down, change its tone, and emit a quiet sound like the chanting in church. Then something would crackle a little inside it and, squeaking one last time, it would fall silent by the stove grate.

Often, one or even two of the village women would come by and spend some time with Darya. Surgan, so bent over that it looked as if she'd been broken in half, would drop in once in a while. One time the women brought a pot of whey not fed to the livestock, another leftover soup from the bottom of their family pot. Surgan treated her to flat cakes made from clover flowers, tasted and praised Darya's cookies, and drank a cup or two of hot boiled water. They would sit for hours by the samovar, telling their dreams to one another, each complaining about her ailments.

Perhaps two or three times over the summer, old man Misha, gray, with his Apostlelike head also visited her. One time he tightened the handle of the oven fork, another he tied with cord the old cracked handle of the scythe.

Each time, they'd ask if there wasn't a letter from Ivan. And when they learned that none had come, they would click their tongues sadly and compassionately. To console Darya they'd say, "A letter will come, Darya dear. Why not? It's got to come. Judge for yourself. There's such a war on now. All sorts of people, ours and others, are all mixed up in it. And the mail as well. Naturally, it, too, sometimes lags behind."

"You're right, dear, you're right," Darya would cheerfully agree and blot her eyes with her apron.

"What's more, now take these bombings. Y'know, how many of these special mail *ashalons* don't get to where they're headed. You couldn't even count 'em all. As for Ivan himself, it may just be that sometimes he just doesn't have nothing to write with, no pencil, not a scrap o' paper. After all, my dear, he's not at home."

"No, he's not home. He's not home, dear."

"If they've been hauled to a huge fiery battle, them,

our boys, wouldn't even have time to have a bite, much less write a letter."

Darya herself did not visit other people in the village.

Once in the morning when it was obvious that a thunderstorm was approaching and that the hay had to be put in stacks quickly, it suddenly occurred to Darya that she might have left the samovar uncovered. The lightening was already flashing right over the village; the storm cloud pressed down on roofs, which turned white in the flashes. Darya ran home, exhausting all her remaining strength in the process. At each clap of thunder, she crossed herself. She kept cursing herself for not covering the samovar with the tablecloth and for leaving the stove damper open.

Darya had just managed to rush into her hut when heavy, dense rain poured down on the village. Thunder resounded all over the heavens. The corners of her darkened hut were lighted up by smoky yellow streaks of lightening. Growing weak from fright, Darya shut the damper and covered the samovar tightly with the linen tablecloth. Just then came such a bang that, before she had time to cross herself, Darya lost her strength and fell to the floor, passing out.

Just as fast as it had come, the storm passed, though thunder continued to roll slowly out beyond the ridge of trees, and golden drops still flew out of the sky as the sun reemerged. Darya was barely able to get out onto the stoop. She felt giddy and her legs would not obey her. She looked fondly at the fresh grass washed by the rain, listened to the chirping of the white-breasted swallows, and cursed herself again: she'd not had the sense to put the tub under the eaves. Despite her weakness and the dull pain in her head, she couldn't help reproaching herself for failing to do this. Suddenly very quietly, soundlessly, she began to whisper something to herself. She felt strange, as if she weren't herself, but someone else, and that this other Darya was reprimanding her for not putting out the tub. It was pleasant, gratifying for her to look at and listen to herself—as if her own body were separated from her. This made her feel weightless and joyful.

In the distance the thunder had begun to fade. From the bright clean grass rose warm bright steam. High above, almost tangible, arched a complete bright rainbow. Wide and clean multicolored bands girded a huge half-circle and dropped into a green field where, screened by these bands, the osier grove shone pearly and pink. It was as if Darya wanted to remember something but could not. What caught her eye was an old, old basket with one flat side, which hung in the entryway on a wooden peg. Looking at this basket, Darya tried long and hard to remember something.

She got onto her feet and, as if sleepwalking, took the basket down and, weakly holding onto the wall of the cowshed, went into the vegetable garden. She opened the bolt and approached the potato patch. The plants were already leafing out. For Darya it was pleasant to look at their pulpy, juicy stems, at the wide rough leaves which were about to adorn themselves with yellowy-white flowers.

Darya got down on her knees. With trembling hands, she dug into the soil, groping for and tearing from the roots the seed potato that fed life to those green stems.

The young potatoes had not even begun to show themselves on the tender, white roots; this Darya saw.

She dug up yet another bush, and then another, laying the black, withered uprooted old potato cuts that she had set out herself into the flat-sided basket. Darya counted ten potato pieces, wiped them on the grass, and then returned to her hut, quiet and contented.

The samovar stood by the stove grate merry and bright, as if waiting for a holiday. Slowly, Darya brought a bucket of water from the well and split off five or so splints from a log. But, before she had a chance to ready them for lighting, The Gimp noisily entered the hut.

"Is the woman of the house at home?"

"She's here, my friend. She's here. Come in, Pasha dear, and sit down."

Darya offered him her small stool. But Pavel the Gimp would not sit on the stool offered him. Instead, he sat on the large bench by the table. Without looking at Darya, he opened his map case and began to go through the papers in it. Darya watched deferentially as he did this. Then Pavel deftly sharpened his pencil with a small knife.

"What 'bout it, Comrade Rumyantseva? Are we gonna to pay up or not? You're the only one in the whole village who is mischievously holding out. It's clear that measures will have to be taken."

"The trouble, Pasha dear, is that I don't have any money right now. Be kind and wait just a little longer."

"No, I don't intend to wait any longer."

"You don't intend to?"

"No, under no circumstances."

Darya went silent and, with a sigh, for some reason or other scraped the table board with the tip of her finger. In businesslike fashion, Pavel looked over the hut and said: "I will sequester something . . . ."

"Y'know what you have to . . . If . . . it's really your business, my friend."

Painstakingly, Pavel wrote out some sort of legal document on a sheet of paper, taking care to make a carbon copy. Darya waited patiently while he did this. Then the two of them walked about the house. Pavel himself opened up the storeroom and, while Darya stood by the doors, he opened the large, ash wicker basket and looked under the small bench. It was dark in the storeroom, and again and again he struck matches.

"So, a basket, an old sieve. That's not what's wanted. A weaving reed. That won't do. What else is there?"

"There are other things, Pasha dear, there are. There's an empty kerosene bottle and yarn, nine skeins of it."

"I'm not asking about that," said Pavel scornfully. "Do you have clothing of any kind or linen?"

"No such thing, old friend. Over there are some two pounds and a quarter of raw wool. Wanted to make some felt boots for winter."

"Where?"

"Over there, old friend, there." Darya gave him the wool that was packed into an old cotton pillow case.

Nothing else interested Pavel. Nothing in the storeroom or in the garret or in the dark cellar that smelled of rot. He went back into the hut, opened the cupboard, examined the sleeping shelf above the stove and the chest next to it, and opened the trapdoor in the floor by its ring, but there was nothing anywhere.

"Here, Comrade Rumyantseva, sign the statement and the verification of sequestration."

"I'm not really educated, Pasha dear."

Pavel knew, even before Darya said this, that she wasn't able to sign her name. One after the other, he pulled on his box calf boots by the tabs on their tops, put the papers in his map case, and once again, without looking at Darya, pronounced with a severe tone in his voice, "That's it, Comrade Rumyantseva!"

Darya poured water into the samovar and wanted to light a few splints with one of Pavel's matches, but Pavel moved the match toward himself, lit up, and extinguished the flame. Darya understood nothing. Only when Pavel took the samovar and proceeded to pour out the water did she begin to cry, saying as she ran in front of him, "Pasha! Dear Pashenka, how can I do without my samovar. Take that wool there. Leave . . . leave the samovar. I'll pray for you as long as I live, Pasha."

But Pavel took away both the wool and the samovar, and in tears Darya sat down on the bench. Once again her head began to swim, aching severely at the top. Without the samovar, the hut lost all is coziness and became forlorn. Darya cried, but the tears in her eyes stopped coming.

Daylight showed through the hut's window for a long time. Far beyond the woods thunder rumbled disturbingly until late in the night. Gadflies flew into the hut, buzzed a little, and flew out again. Some would knock against the window, bumping for hours on the glass of the frames with their foreheads and, tired out, grow silent.

Darya heard none of this. She gnawed on a raw soft seed potato she'd dug out of the earth. She gnawed one more and lay down on the stove. Not aware whether it was day or night, morning or evening, she lay on the stove sensing that her arms and legs were growing weak.

Over and over again she tried to separate dream from reality, but couldn't do it at all. And the faraway thunder seemed to her to be the sound of an extended war taking place in two battle zones. Darya imagined war to consist of two endless rows of soldiers carrying rifles. It seemed as though the soldiers stood in rows, one opposite the other, one Russian, the other German, and that they were taking turns shooting at each another. Between the rows of Russians and Germans lay even green grass. The rows of soldiers were disappearing far beyond the horizon, and it seemed as though the soldiers fired at one another in turns. And Ivan, her son, was standing in full sight of everyone, on a small rise. For some reason he had no rifle in his hands. Darya was seized with fear. It seemed to her that he was about to be slain because he was standing unarmed. She wanted terribly to shout to him that he should grab a rifle fast, but no sound came out of her mouth. In a state of anguish, Darya ran to him. She wanted to run faster, but her legs wouldn't obey. Something heavy and all-powerful stopped her from reaching her son. And the rows of soldiers moved away from Darya slowly and inevitably, receding farther and farther away.

Two or three days later Surgan went to the store to buy a whetstone for sharpening scythes and saw Darya's samovar on the counter. In her astonishment, she even tried its faucet: the samovar was indeed Darya's.

"Oh my, oh my! They've really taken it away from her," thought Surgan. "That devil Gimp, took the samovar away from the old woman."

During the mowing, Surgan told the other women that she had seen Darya's samovar on the counter in the store. The women began to moan, pitying Darya. Then they realized that Darya had not come to the fields for three days, and they all became more and more alarmed.

"And just how much do they want for it?"

"Darya now, do y'think she's still alive, girls?"

"That Gimp, that Gimp, it's just the sort of thing his type would do."

"He's a dog, not a man, a dog. . . ."

"We should redeem that samovar, we should," observed someone, and the women grew quiet, frightened by this proposition. But then one after another they again began to moan, talking on and on. And it just happened somehow that they decided that there was only one thing to be done: the whole village should take up a collection and redeem the samovar.

Because it was the mowing season, the store stayed open in the evening. The women collected as much as people could afford, redeemed the samovar, and, satisfied with themselves, went together to Darya's hut. However, the lock that didn't work was hanging at the gate, and in the latch was stuck the small birch stick.

"It's clear that our dear friend has left, has gone and

become a beggar," said Surgan. They opened the gates and walked around the empty house. Everything was swept clean, the wardrobe was closed, and the oven prongs were standing in orderly fashion by the stove. Surgan was quick to notice that the basket with one flat side was not in the room nor in the small entrance hall.

The women placed the samovar in its usual place, sighed, and left, locking up the gate as they'd found it.

"Gone to wander 'bout the whole wide world."

"Perhaps good Christian folk will not abandon her."

"To be single is not bad, but when it is bad, only you know."

"That's for sure."

"They say you shouldn't think y'can avoid poverty or prison," said Surgan, as she put the very same birch stick back into the latch on Darya's gate. "God willing, the war will come to an end, and life will return to normal again."

The haymaking followed its ordinary course.

During the summer hundreds of beggars passed through the village: old men, children, old women. But no one saw Darya even once. Her hut stood deserted. Her little patch of potatoes behind the hut had bloomed and faded, and a dozen or so wooden shingles that had begun to rot had slipped off the roof in the yard. As for Darya herself, she didn't come back to the village.

The old women would ask the beggars if they hadn't seen Darya, if they hadn't met her somewhere, but no one had seen her, no one had run into her.

Only when winter had already come did a rumor one day reach the village that they'd found the corpse of an old woman in a pile of hay in a forest clearing about ten kilometers away. Someone had driven in there for the hay and found her. It seemed like she'd been there since autumn, because the pieces of bread in her basket were all dried up and she was wearing summer clothing. The women unanimously concluded that this had to be their Darya. Who else they said could it be except her? But old Misha simply laughed at the women. "The way you've guessed is like blowing into a puddle," he said. "You think this can't be anyone else than our old woman Darya, huh? Ain't there more than a few old women like her in old Mother Ru-u-ssie? If you had to count these old women, come on, really, there wouldn't be numbers enough. And you keep saying, 'Darya, it's Darya!' Those old women, there's so many of 'em. . . ."

The women waved Misha away, holding firm to their opinion, "You, Mikhailo, sit and don't argue. Darya was in the pile of hay, couldn't be anyone else."

Misha brushed them off, "May God forgive you, you magpies. Can anyone ever outargue you?"

And to be sure, for a single old man to argue with the women was hopeless. But perhaps they were right, these women. Who knows? Women do almost always turn out to be right, especially when there's that kind of war going on.

VASILY BELOV

THE BURIAL
GROUND

He woke up with some sort of vague, nagging anxiety. He looked at the bright, intense sunbeam penetrating the far end of the log barn, and tried to understand where this disturbing yet somehow pleasant emotional pain had come from. He tried to recall what he'd been dreaming about, but the images of the night's dreams eluded him, leaving him with a dissatisfied feeling.

The sun also beat in through the narrow gaps between the logs. Swallows flew in the window with a whistlelike sound. They pressed their graceful tails to the rafters, twittered, and then flew out again. There was a smell of green grass and of evaporating dew. In the stream somewhere, small children, bathing since early morning, were shouting, and in the field a horse-drawn mowing machine chirred.

No one was in the house. His mother, as was her life-long habit, had gone to mow the hay, doubtless with an old woman's moans and groans. His wife and two kids had gone, as they did every morning, to a distant pond to sun and swim.

Yesterday's meeting with a friend in the village—a friend his age—came to mind, and suddenly he understood the reason for his anguish. Yesterday he hadn't realized fully how old, how aged this childhood friend looked. Yet he himself was even older than the friend, and last night in a dream he experienced a feeling of the irreversible. . . . Up till then he'd thought of himself as being young, but there in the subconscious world of his dream he suddenly understood that his youth had actually come to an end long ago, and that he'd begun to live out the second half of his life. "Live out"—what a strange expression that was.

No one was in the village. Just as it was in his childhood during the haymaking season, thin sticks were by the gates of the houses, and a few martins and swallows cut through the blue of the warm air over the roofs. The morning sun had already heated the soft dust of the street.

He went out into the green field ringing with the sound of grasshoppers, and, as he went, he slowly took in the very familiar surroundings and the villages he'd not seen for many years. He felt now he belonged to all this and was surprised by that somehow strangely joyous yet sad feeling: Where'd he come from and what did all this mean? Where was the source who gave him life back then, say perhaps four hundred years ago? Where were all his forebears now and what did it mean that they weren't here anymore? Was it possible that all that was left of them now was him and his two sons? It was strange, hard to comprehend.

He reached the steep, green knoll, girded by a pale blue horseshoe-shaped lake. The church dome floated in the sky, floated on occasional white clouds, floated but couldn't drift away. Bees buzzed softly over clumps of willows. Below in the breeze and sunlight the lake glimmered, its blue surface pierced by the rays of the sun seemed now to break, then darken, changing incessantly. Here on the knoll it was peaceful and green. The sultry air rose up into the sky, distorting the forested horizon with its wavy vertical currents. In contrast to the gray, thin crosses that seemed tipsy from time, the new fence gleamed white, and the arch of the new pine gate floated in the sky together with the dome of the church.

He wandered about the knoll for a long time, searching for graves and not finding them, pushing his way through strong young burdock. The grave of an aunt turned out to be far beyond the fence. He recognized it from the stone. But just where was it that his grandma lay? He recalled that his grandmother's grave was near some willows, but he could find nothing whatsoever and sat down on someone else's grave, a grave quite fresh. Now what's the point of looking for the graves of four great-grandmothers if you can't even find your own grandmother's grave? He knew that his other grandmother, his father's mother, was buried here somewhere. But where? There wasn't even a hint of where it was. Everything was level with the ground and overgrown with grass and burdock.

Suddenly, a simple, clear thought startled him, made him clench his teeth. It'd never occurred to him before: here in the place where he was born and grew up, even the cemetery was only for women. He suddenly realized that there wasn't a single man from his family in this burial ground. They, the men, were born here, on this land, yet not one returned to it, as if shunning the company of women and this green burial ground. Generation after generation they'd gone off somewhere. Obviously, it didn't take them long to give up the rake for a rifle, the haying shirt for a soldier's blouse. They went, hurrying, as if to a fair—almost immediately after they'd built a house and produced sons. And now, here in their homeland, lonely even in their graves, lay great-grandmothers and grandmothers.

He lit up a cigarette. For the first time ever, the picture on the box made him remember that one of his forebears had perished in Bulgaria during the war with the Turks. His grandmother used to talk about this. And with bitter irony, he began to think about the injustices of that woman's fate: even in death his great-grandfather had been lucky. Maybe over his grave an obelisk had been erected, put there by the Bulgarians commemorating the glorious heroes of Shipka. While he couldn't even find his great-grandmother's grave.

He thought about how fate also had been kind to his grandfather. Certainly, it was more pleasant to lie in a Manchurian burial ground when it's a burial ground immortalized in novels and stories, when it's a burial ground depicted in battle paintings hanging in museums, where crowds of descendants of the heroes gather round, and when sad waltzes about Manchurian burial grounds are heard on the radio. While his grandmother's grave had disappeared; there was neither a cross nor a stone to be seen anywhere.

He put out his cigarette, but then lit another. Why?

Hell, now take his father. His father had outdone them all, even his grandfather and great-grandfather. There's no mightier monument in the whole world than the one there on Mamaev Hill. He remembered how last summer he was in Volgograd and how he had walked all day on Mamaev Hill. The grave which had taken his father into its depths was monumental and sad. The enormous sculpture crowning its top cast a gigantic shadow over the city. In the hall celebrating military valor, work was still going on, but nonetheless he, the son of a sergeant who had perished on the Volga, had found his family name engraved on the granite wall.

They went away. They all went away, protected by monuments in great burial grounds. His grandfathers and great-grandfathers went away, his father went away. And not a single one returned to their native green burial ground, skirted by the golden horseshoe-shaped lake, where their wives and mothers lay. No one brings flowers to this spot, no one visits these women to comfort them in their loneliness, a loneliness which persists even in death.

He sat on the green, peaceful, hot rise under a willow and thought about this. Perhaps his turn also would come one day. Would he go the way of his male ancestors, to strange, foreign burial grounds?

VASILY SHUKSHIN

I WANNA

LIVE

A clearing on a hummock, in the clearing there'll be a small log hut. Nothing special, just a shed, walls thirteen or fourteen logs high with one small window, no porch, and sometimes no roof. Who since the beginning of time has built these huts in the taiga? There're people who come in the springtime, fell pine trees roughly equal in size and debark them. Later, during those fine days of early fall, three or four axes will be at work for a week or so, putting up a hut. From clay and stones found nearby a small crude stove will be thrown together. Stick a chimney out through the roof, knock together a plank bed . . . and live to your heart's content!

Going into one of these small huts in wintertime, it doesn't seem like anyone's lived there. On the walls and in the crevices there's rime as thick as your palm, and the dank smell of stagnant smoke.

But then the firewood begins to crackle in the stove, you take in the heavy damp smell of thawing clay, the walls drip, there are strong fumes. The best thing to do is stoke up the stove, go outside for a while, and chop more wood for later on. In half an hour the hut's warmer and easier to be in. You can slip out of your fur jacket and stuff the stove until it's full again. The walls will still be steaming a little, the stove raging hot. A peaceful bliss, a certain joy comes over you. "Ah!" you want to say, "This is just perfect." It's dry almost everywhere now, but the boards of the plank bed are still cold. No need to worry about that; they'll warm up soon. For the time being, you can throw your fur jacket on them, stick your grub sack under your head, and point your feet toward the stove. Drowsiness comes over you—you nearly succumb. You don't feel like getting up and throwing more wood on the fire. But you gotta.

By now there's a whole mound of fiery red coals in the stove. Logs catch fire immediately, like birch bark. Right in front of the stove there's a block of wood. You can sit on it, smoke—and think. When you're alone, you think better. It's dark except for the light coming from the cracks in the stove which plays about the floor, the walls, and the ceiling. God knows what'll come to mind. You may suddenly recall the first time you walked a girl home. How you walked next to her and said nothing, like a dummy. You're sitting there grinning and you don't even know it. What the hell. It's great!

Now it's really warm. You can make some tea. Brick tea, the green stuff. Smells like grass, reminds you of summer.

This is how it was one evening in the twilight as old Nikitich sat in front of such a stove sucking on his favorite pipe.

It was hot in the hut, but outside it was freezing. Nikitich felt at peace with the world. He'd roamed the taiga since he was little. There he plied his trade, hunting squirrel and occasionally killing a staggering winter bear. This is why he always kept five or six shells loaded with buckshot in the left pocket of his fur jacket. He loved the taiga, especially in the winter. Stillness so great you felt its weight a little. But solitude doesn't oppress, it gives you a sense of freedom. Nikitich would squint, look around, fully aware he was the sole owner of this great white kingdom.

Nikitich sat and smoked.

Outside skis scraped the snow, then all was quiet. It seemed like someone had peeped in the little window. Then came the scraping sound of skis again, coming up to the stoop. Two knocks on the door with one of the poles.

"Anybody there?"

A young voice, hoarse from the cold, not that of a man who knows how to talk with himself, and then a long silence.

Couldn't be a hunter, Nikitich knew. A hunter doesn't go asking questions, he comes right in.

"Yep."

The man outside the door took his skis off, leaned them against the wall; he made one of the steps creak. The door opened slightly and, in the white cloud of steam, Nikitich could barely make out a tall guy wearing a belted, quilted jacket, wadded pants, and an old soldier's cap.

"Who's there?"

"Me." Nikitich lighted a splint and raised it up over his head. For a while they looked at one another in silence.

"You alone?"

"Yeah."

The young guy went over to the stove, took off his mittens, stuck them under his arm, and stretched his hands toward the grate.

"What cold, shit. . . ."

"Real cold." Only now did Nikitich notice that the young guy had no rifle. No, this was no hunter. Didn't look like one. Not the right face or clothes. "March. March is still making itself felt."

"How come March. It's April!"

"New Style, but according to the old calendar it's March. We say: 'March, March, two britches with starch.' You aren't wearing much." About his not having a rifle the old man said nothing.

"Don't worry about it," said the young guy. "You alone here?"

"Yeah. You already asked that."

The young guy didn't react.

"Sit down. I'll put some tea on."

"Let me warm up a little first." The young guy's accent wasn't local, a Russian but not from hereabouts. This piqued the old man's curiosity, but age-old custom—not asking too many questions right away—was stronger than his curiosity.

The young guy warmed up his hands, then lighted a cigarette. "You got it good here. It's warm."

When he lit up, Nikitich got a better look at him. A handsome pale face with thick eyelids. He inhaled greedily, opening his mouth slightly. Two gold front teeth glittered. Unshaved. A small neat beard, curling slightly on his cheeks. Emaciated. He noticed that the old man was observing him. Raising the half-burned match, he looked closely at the old man. He threw away the match. His look stuck in Nikitich's mind: no-nonsense, bold. And somehow "cool," as Nikitich would say. For no reason he thought: "The type girls like."

"Sit down. What are you standing there for?"

The young guy smiled. "That's not the way you say it, Pops. You supposed to say 'Take a seat.'"

"Then take a seat. What'ya mean not the way you say it? That's what we say here."

"I'll sit down anyway. No one else coming?"

"Who's supposed to come? It's late. If anybody comes, there'll be room." Nikitich moved over on the wooden block, the young guy sat down next to him, and again stretched his hands toward the fire. His hands weren't those of a working man, though the young guy obviously was fit. Nikitich liked his smile, not impudent, guileless, or restrained. But then there were those gold teeth. A handsome guy. Shave off that beard, put on a decent suit—a teacher. Nikitich really liked teachers.

"Some sort of 'ologist?" he asked.

"A what?"

"Y'know, one of those who do prospecting in the taiga."

"O-Oh. Yeah . . . that's me."

"How come you don't have a gun? Risky."

"Got separated from my group," the young guy said reluctantly. "Your village far away?"

"'Bout a hundred fifty versts."

The young guy nodded, closed his eyes slightly, and sat that way a while, enjoying the warmth. Then he roused himself and sighed.

"Tired."

"Been wandering a long time by yourself?"

"A long time. Got anything to drink?"

"I can find something."

The young guy livened up. "Great! I'm chilled to the bone. You could freeze your ass off. You call this April?"

Nikitich went outside and got a small bag of pork fat. He lit the lantern hanging from the ceiling.

"They oughta teach you a little 'bout how to be on your own in the taiga. But all they do is send you here, and how're you supposed to know? Now just last year I found one . . . he'd thawed out in the spring. Young, too. Also had a beard. Wrapped himself up in a blanket . . . and that was it, kicked the bucket." Nikitich cut the pork fat on the edge of the plank bed. "But turn me loose in the taiga and I can survive by myself all winter with no trouble. As long as I have shells . . . and matches."

"Still you crawl into this hut."

"Yah. Since it's here, why I should sack out in the snow? I'm not my own enemy."

The young guy undid his belt and took off his quilted jacket. He walked back and forth in the hut. Broadshouldered, imposing. He'd already warmed up, his look had softened, clearly he was damned glad he'd happened upon a warm place, found a living person. He lit up another cigarette. His cigarettes smelled good.

Nikitich loved to talk with city people, though he

was scornful of them for their helplessness in the taiga. Sometimes he'd get the chance to earn extra money guiding some prospecting party. Inwardly, he'd laugh at them, but he loved to listen to their conversation and liked talking with them. It made him feel good when they chatted with him indulgently, condescendingly chuckling now and again. However, leave them to themselves and it'd be another matter; they'd perish like blind sucklings. It was even more interesting when there were two or three gals in the group. They put up with things, didn't complain. It was always as if they were same as the men—didn't want anyone to help them. They'd all sleep together. And nothing would happen . . . nobody'd misbehave. Put country people in their place, and you'd never be able to guard against sin. But with these people, nothing happened. Y'know, some of the gals were a feast for the eyes. One of them would put on tight pants, a close-fitting blouse, tie a scarf on against the midges, nice 'n' round . . . a doll, a perfect doll. But the guys wouldn't react, as if all this was perfectly normal.

"What are you looking for?"

"Where?"

"Y'know, when you come here."

The young guy smiled to himself. "My fate."

"Your fate. . . . It's like an eel, my friend, slippery. You think you've grabbed it, it's in your hands, but it was never really there."

Nikitich was in the mood for a good talk. As usual when he was with city people, he'd speak fancifully when he sensed they were following him closely—when they listened to him and exchanged glances with one another, one of them getting interested enough maybe even to write something down in a notebook. Nikitich could easily discourse this way all night. All you had to do was listen. His own people, from the village, would dismiss him as a chotterer, but these people would listen. Real nice. Sometimes he'd think to himself: "I really know how to string things together, dammit!" He knew how to spin the kind of yarn the priest used to give you in the old days. He'd say that the trees in the forest had souls: "Don't touch them, don't chop them with an ax when there's no need," he would say, "for that'll make them dry up, and when they dry up, you'll dry up yourself. You'll be overcome by sadness and you'll dry up, and you'll never guess why." Or this: "From the city many folk come with rifles and shoot left and right. Bang, bang! Doesn't matter where and what they hit. Female, male—don't matter as long as they kill something. For doing such things their hands oughta be pulled off. You killed her, a female bear, and she had two cubs. They'll die. Now you've got one pelt, but if you'd waited a little, there'd be three. Amusing yourself at the expense of a wild beast makes no sense."

"That's fate for you," continued Nikitich out loud.

Except that the young guy was in no mood for listening. He went over to the window and peered a long time out into the darkness. Then, as if waking up, he said, "Just the same, it'll soon be spring."

"It'll come 'cause it has nowhere else to go. Sit down. Let's have something to eat from what God has given us."

They melted some snow in a pot, diluted some alcohol, and had a drink. They ate some frozen pork fat with it. This made them feel really good. Nikitich threw more wood into the stove. The young guy again was drawn to the window. He made a little circle on the pane with his breath and kept looking out into the night.

"What d'ya think you gonna see out there now?" Nikitich asked, wondering out loud. He wanted to talk.

"Freedom," said the young guy, and he sighed. But the sigh wasn't sad and the word freedom had a firm, angry, and assertive tone. He swung back from the window.

"Give me some more, Pops." He undid the collar of his black sateen shirt, and with his wide palm gave his chest a resounding blow and rubbed. "My soul needs a drink."

"You should eat first, or your empty stomach'll throw you for a loop."

"No, it won't. It won't throw me." And, affectionately and tightly hugging the old man by the neck, he began to sing:

> And on death row
> In a cell damp and cold,
> A hoary old man did appear . . .

He then smiled affectionately. The young guy's eyes burned with a bright, joyous glow.

"Let's drink, my good man!"

"You got bored being alone so long," and Nikitich smiled as well. He liked the young guy more and more. Young, strong, handsome. He could have been done for. "You know, buddy, you could have been done for. No rifle in the taiga is a pretty bad business."

"We won't be done for, Pops. We're goin' to live it up!"

He said this, again firmly, and for an instant his eyes looked somewhere far, far away and again became cold. You couldn't figure out what he was thinking. It was as if he recalled something, but that something wasn't what he wanted to recall. He tossed off the glass, draining it to the bottom in one swig. He cleared his throat loudly, twirled his head. He chewed some pork fat. He lighted a cigarette. He stood up, unable to stay seated. He paced back and forth with long strides. He stopped in the middle of the hut, put his hands on his hips, and again fixed his eyes on something far away.

"I wanna live, Pops."

"Everyone wants to live. You think I don't want to? And I don't have much longer . . . "

"I wanna live!" repeated the big handsome guy stubbornly and with a joyous anger, ignoring the old man. "You don't know her, life. She's . . . " He thought a little, and clenched his teeth, "She's a beaut, a sweetie, I wan' her for my very own!"

Nikitich, who had become tipsy, giggled. "You tal' 'bout life jus' like ya would 'bout a woman."

"Women are cheap stuff." The young guy was now aglow with some stubborn, daring, exhilarating feeling. He wouldn't listen to the old man. *He* was talking, and he wanted the old man to listen to him now. The powerful force of the young guy began to egg the old man on.

"Women, they . . . of course. But without 'em. . . ."

"We'll take hold of her, the beaut," he said, thrusting his hands out and clenching his fists. "We'll grab this sweetie by her soft neck. . . . D'ya remember Nicky the professor? Forgot me?" Now the young guy was talking with some woman, and was quite amazed that he'd been "forgotten." "*That* Nicky! But Nicky remembers you. Nicky hasn't forgotten you." He either was rejoicing or he intended to wreak vengeance on someone. "But I . . . here I am. I beg you, madam, may I exchange a few tender words with you? I won't offend you. But you will give me back everything. Everything! I'm gonna take it from you!"

"Did a woman really stir you up that much?" asked Nikitich amazed.

The young guy shook his head.

"That woman's called 'Freedom.' You don't know her either, Pops. You're an unsophisticated man, an animal. You're happy here. But you don't know big city lights. Those lights beckon. There are kind, good people there. They have it warm and soft, and music plays. They're polite, and very afraid of death. And when I walk about the city, it's all mine. Why is it they're there and I'm here? Savvy?"

"You're not gonna be here forever."

"You don't savvy." The young guy was speaking seriously, sternly. "I oughta be there because I'm not afraid of anyone. I'm not afraid of death, and that means that life is mine."

The old man shook his head. "I don't get it, buddy. What're ya talking about?"

The young guy went over to the plank bed and filled their glasses. Suddenly he seemed tired. "I'm running away from prison, Pops," he said without any expression. "Shall we drink?"

Nikitich automatically clinked his glass against the young guy's. The young guy drank up. He looked at the old man . . . who was still holding his glass in his hand. The old man looked up at him.

"What's the matter?"

"What'ya mean?"

"Drink," ordered the young guy. He wanted to smoke some more, but was out of cigarettes. "Gimme yours."

"All I got is shag."

"That'll do."

They had a smoke. The young guy sat down on the block, closer to the fire. There was a long silence.

"They'll catch you in the end," said Nikitich. It wasn't exactly that he felt sorry for the young guy, but suddenly he pictured him, strong, handsome, being led away under guard. He felt sorry for the young guy's youth, his handsomeness and strength. They'll nab him. It'll be . . . all turned into shit. No one'll be either better or worse for his good looks. What good were they? "Won't do you no good," he said soberly.

"What'ya talking about?"

"You running away. Nowadays ain't the way it used to be. They'll catch you."

The young guy didn't answer. He looked pensively at the fire. He bent over and tossed a piece of wood into the stove.

"Should've stayed in prison your whole term. No good running."

"Stop that!" The young guy cut him short. In some strange way he'd sobered up. "I've got a mind of my own."

"No doubt about that," agreed Nikitich. "Got far to go?"

"Be quiet for a while."

"Must have a mother and father," mused Nikitich looking at the back of the young guy's head. "He'll come home and make them happy, the son of a bitch."

They were silent for five minutes or so. The old man knocked the ashes out of his pipe and tamped it again. The young guy kept staring at the fire.

"Your village . . . is it a district center or not?" he asked not turning round.

"District center? That's another ninety versts from here. You'll be done for. It's still wintertime in the taiga. . . ."

"I'll stay with you about three days. To regain some of my strength." He didn't ask, just said it.

"Fine, I don't mind. So, you still had a long time to go in prison and couldn't take it anymore?"

"A long time."

"What did they put you in for?"

"Don't ever ask anyone a question like that, Pops."

Nikitich puffed away on his pipe, which was dying out—revived it, inhaled, and had a fit of coughing. He said, coughing, "Makes no difference to me. I'm just sorry. They'll get you."

"As long as God's with you, no asshole's gonna do you in. Won't be easy to get me. Let's get some sleep."

"Lie down. I'll wait 'til the wood has burned up, then close the flue. Otherwise we'll be frozen stiff by morning."

The young guy spread his quilted jacket on the plank bed. With his eyes he sought something to put under his head. He spotted Nikitich's rifle on the wall. He went and took it down, looked it over, hung it back up. "Ancient."

"So? Still works. Over there in the corner there's a felt pad. Spread it under you, and roll up your jacket for your head. Put your feet out that way, toward the stove. By morning it'll be cold anyway."

The young guy spread out the felt, stretched out, and sighed loudly. "Tashkent is small potatoes," he said, God only knows why. "Are you afraid of me, Pops?"

"You?" said the old man amazed. "Why should I be afraid of you?"

"Well . . . I'm an escapee from a prison camp. Maybe I was there for murder."

"For murder, God'll punish you, not men. Y'can keep running away from people, but Him you can't escape."

"You're a believer, are you? An Old Believer probably."

"Old Believer! Now would an Old Believer drink vodka with you?"

"True. But don't go and try to teach me about those gods of yours. . . . They make me sick." The young guy was speaking casually, his voice rather flat. "If I ran into this Christ of yours somewhere, I'd rip his guts out on the spot."

"For what?"

"For what? . . . For telling fairy tales, for lying, that's what. Good people don't exist! Your goody-goody Jesus taught people to suffer patiently. What shit!" The young guy's voice had again begun to take on that firm and angry quality. Except now his voice had no cheer in it. "Who's good?! Me? You?"

"I, for one, during my whole 'ife never did nobody any harm."

"Don't you kill animals? Did He teach that you should do that?"

"You can't tell your prick from a finger. A person's one thing, an animal's another."

"Both are living creatures. Don't you guys say this over and over? You're all scum."

Nikitich couldn't actually see the young guy's face, but he could still picture it . . . pale, with a neat beard. In the warm quiet of the hut, the fierce voice of the man with a face so good and so handsome, who had been hopelessly battered by fate, sounded wild and absurd.

"Why did you get so sore at me?"

"Don't you lie! Don't deceive other people, you hypocrites. They taught you to suffer patiently? Then suffer! The way things are now, before one of you has finished praying you pull down your pants and grab a broad, you lowlife. If it were up to me, I'd invent a new Christ right now, one who'd teach you to smash someone's puss. You're lying? Take this, you scum!"

"Don't talk filth!" said Nikitich sternly. "I let you in as I would any decent person, and now you've started to curse. You're pissed off 'cause they locked you up. Must've been for something. Who can you blame besides yourself?"

"Hmm." The young guy gritted his teeth. He said nothing.

"I'm not a priest, and this ain't no church where you can come 'n' spit out your anger. This is the taiga where everyone's equal. Keep that in mind. Otherwise you won't reach your freedom, you'll crack your skull open. Y'know what they say: brave in front of a lamb, but a lamb in front of the brave. There's a hard and bad man waitin' somewhere for you. You go 'n' offend him the way you did me, for no good reason at all, and he'll show you where to find your freedom."

"Don't get mad, Pops," said the young guy, becoming conciliatory. "I hate it when they try to teach me how to live. Makes my blood boil. They shove all sorts of slime and worms up your nose and tell you these are the good things, this is how you should live your life. I hate that!" He was nearly shouting. "I won't live like that. They lie! It reeks of death! Clean, washed dead people we all feel sorry for, we all love, but you should learn to love the living, the unwashed. There ain't no saints on earth. I ain't seen them. Why keep insisting they exist?!" The young guy raised himself on his elbow. His face showed like a faint white spot in the dim light of the corner. His eyes had an angry and sinister gleam to them.

"When you cool off a little, you'll understand that if there weren't any good people, life would've come to an end long ago. People would've eaten one another or slit one another's throats. This ain't something no Christ taught me, it's my own thought. About saints, that's right, ain't none. I myself am no better than others. No one'll say I'm bad or evil. But when I was young. . . . Not far away was a settlement of Old Believers. On the other side of a marshy plain lived a family, an old man and an old woman and their daughter who was maybe twenty-five. Perhaps they weren't so old, the old folks, but that's the way they seemed to me then, old. Later they moved away. Well, yeah, so they had this daughter. They were as holy as all get out. They moved far away from people so they'd be further from sin, as they liked to say. Yet I lured the daughter one day into a birch grove and . . . then . . . y'know, made it with her. A good lay, a big strong woman. In the end she was expecting a baby, and I was already married. . . ."

"And you say you never did anything bad to anyone?"

"So it turns out I'm no saint. I didn't really force her, did I? Wore her down with tenderness, but it's all the same . . . I all but abandoned the child. When you think about it, you feel sorry. He must be big now. Bet he swears like a trooper."

"You gave life to a human being, you didn't kill him. And maybe you saved her. Maybe she broke with her family after this. Otherwise, they'd driven her crazy with their prayers. She'd have hanged herself on a tree branch somewhere, and that would've been that. And she'd never have known a man. You did a good deed, don't let it bother you."

"Good or bad, it happened. Not much good in it, that's for sure."

"Anything left in there?"

"Likker? There's a little. Drink it. I don't want any more."

The young guy drank it. He cleared his throat again. He didn't eat anything.

"D'ya drink a lot?"

"No, it's . . . I just got so cold. This ain't the way to drink, Pops. You need to have the right atmosphere. Music. Good cigarettes. Champagne. Women. It should be quiet, civilized." Again the young guy was lost in day-dreams. He lay down and stuck his hands behind his head. "I hate dives. Those ain't people, they're animals. Mmmm . . . there are ways to live beautifully! If in one night I flirt seven times with Madame Death . . . so? If she's stroked me with her bony hand and tried to kiss me on the forehead, that exhausts me. Then I rest up. I enjoy and love life more than all the public prosecutors put together. You talk about danger? I have to agree with you. But even if my soul dies within me, even if it shakes like a lamb's tail, I go straight on. I won't stumble and I won't turn back."

"What did'ya do before?" Nikitich was curious.

"Me? I was a supplier. I was an agent for cultural exchanges with foreign countries. As a matter of fact, I was a scientist, a senior lecturer on 'What the Colorado Beetle Is and How to Fight It.'" The young guy went silent, and after a minute in a sleepy voice said, "That's it, Pops . . . I'm out."

"Get some sleep then."

Nikitich stirred the fire with a short poker, filled his pipe, and began thinking about the young guy. See what life had done to him. Had everything you could want: good looks, health, some brains . . . . And what happened? What's in store for him? Running around in the forest. No doubt about it, the city is what brings them to no good. They all go mad there. Nikitich's grandsons—all three of them—also live in a large city. Two are studying, one works and is married. They don't boast like this one, but they're drawn to the city. When they come in the summer, they're bored. Nikitich gets them rifles, takes them into the taiga, and waits for them to brighten up, feel renewed, air all the learning out of their brains. They pretend to feel good, and this makes Nikitich uneasy, since he has nothing more to entertain his grandsons with. It's hard on him because he feels he's disappointed them. The only thing they have on their minds is the city.

Now this young guy on the plank bed, he's also hell-bent on getting to the city. What someone in his situation needs to do is go somewhere far, far away, make a hide-out for himself, and lie low for about five years, if he can't stand being in prison anymore. But he's heading right back where they can grab you by the scruff of the neck at every turn. He knows this, but he's going anyway. "What power the city must have. So, OK, I'm an old man. I was there three times in all. So I don't understand. I agree it's fun there and there're lots of lights. But since I don't understand, I don't bad-mouth it either. If you want to be there, good for you. As for me, I like it here. But why is it they have to come here and turn up their noses. "It's boring. It's dull." Now you should take a really close look. Before you've had a chance to see a thing, you're already jabbering away about your city. But you'd better take a good look, for example, at how the ant lives, or the mole. Or any other living creature. And look because you're interested. Then ask yourself how much you know about life. You tell me tall tales about the city, but if I begin to tell you all I know. . . . But they don't listen to me. You they gape at because you're from the city. I don't give a fart that you live in a city and strut along the sidewalks in fancy shoes. What good has this strutting of yours done you? They must've given you at least fifteen years for this beautiful life of yours. Must've broken into a store, what else? You had your little fling and then came down with a crash. And now this one's asking for trouble again. Of his own free will! So it's pretty clear he can't live without the city. Must have some store again in mind he wants to rob. Champagne. And where'll he get his champagne from? What a bunch of fools. The city'll gobble you up, it will, bones 'n' all. You have to pity them, the fools. But there's nothing you can do. No good arguing with them."

The wood in the stove had burned out. Nikitich waited for the last little sparks to die out in the ashes, closed the flue, put out the lantern, and lay down next to the young guy. The latter breathed deeply and evenly, his arm tucked awkwardly under himself. He didn't even stir when Nikitich straightened his arm.

"All tuckered out," thought Nikitich. "What an ass he is. And what made him do it? What asses they are!"

After midnight, outside, near the hut, there was a noise. Two or three men's voices could be heard.

The young guy sat bolt upright as if he hadn't been asleep. Nikitich also raised his head.

"Who's that?" asked the young guy quickly.

"Damned if I know."

The young guy took off from the plank bed in the direction of the door. He listened, feeling his way along the wall. He was searching for the rifle. Nikitich guessed what he was up to.

"Now don't be a fool!" he cried out quietly. "You'll make things worse."

"Who's that?" the young guy asked again.

"I just told you I don't know."

"Don't let 'em in. Lock the door."

"Don't be stupid. No one locks the door to a hut like

this. There's nothing even to lock it with. Lie down and don't move."

"Now, Gramps. . . ."

The young guy didn't have time to finish what he was saying. Someone was on the stoop and fumbling for the door hook. The young guy slid like a snake onto the plank bed, and managed to whisper, "Pops, I swear by God and the devil and all that is holy, if you betray me. . . . I beg you, old man. I'll be eternally . . . ."

"Keep down," Nikitich ordered.

The door swung open wide. "Ha!" a deep bass voice said cheerfully. "I'd said someone was here. It's warm. Come on in."

"Shut that door," said Nikitich angrily, getting down off the plank bed. "He's glad it's warm! Open it a little more and it'll be good 'n' hot."

"OK," said the bass voice. "It's warm and the owner's cordial."

Nikitich lit the lantern.

Two other men came in. One Nikitich knew. He was the district police chief. All the hunters knew him because he harassed them about hunting licenses and made them pay their fees.

"You're named Emelianov?" asked the police chief, a tall, hefty man around fifty. "Right?"

"Right, Comrade Protokin."

"OK then. Make your guests feel welcome."

The three of them began taking off their coats.

"Doin' some shooting?" asked Nikitich not without irony. He didn't like casual shooters like these guys. All they did was make noise and go away again.

"Gotta loosen up a little. Who's this?" The chief had spotted the young guy on the plank bed.

"An 'ologist," Nikitich explained reluctantly. "Got left behind by his group."

"Got lost, did he?"

"That's it."

"We haven't heard anything about it. Where were they headed to, did he tell you?"

"A lot he says. Hardly opened his mouth, he was so frozen. I filled him up with alcohol and now he's sleeping like a dead man."

The police chief struck a match and held it close to the young guy's face. The latter didn't move a muscle. He breathed evenly.

"You pumped him full." The chief's match burned out. "Wonder why we haven't heard anything?"

"Maybe they didn't get to report it yet?" said one of the others.

"Can't be. Looks like he's been wandering for a long time. Didn't tell you how long he's been on his own?"

"No," replied Nikitich. "Fell behind, he said. And that's all."

"Let'm sleep it off. Tomorrow we'll straighten it all out. What'ya say, guys. Should we get some sleep?"

"Yeah," agreed the two. "Is there room?"

"There's room," said the chief reassuringly. "Last time there were five of us too. We nearly croaked by morning. We'd heated the place up some, but not enough. Must have been close to fifty below outside.

They undressed and lay down on the plank bed.

Nikitich resumed his position next to the young guy. The newcomers talked a little while about district business and then fell silent. Soon everyone was asleep.

Nikitich woke up very early. He could just barely make out the little window in the wall. The young guy wasn't next to him. Nikitich very carefully got down off the plank bed, searched in his pockets for matches. It still hadn't occurred to him that something might be wrong. He struck a match. No sign of the young guy. His quilted jacket was missing along with Nikitich's rifle. There was an ominous twinge in his heart. "He's gone. Took the rifle with him."

He got dressed without making a sound, took one of the three rifles stacked in the corner, and felt in his pocket for the cartridges with buckshot. He opened the door quietly and went out.

Day was just beginning to break. During the night it had got warmer. A foggy mist clouded the faint color of dawn. You couldn't see a thing even five paces away. The smell of spring was in the air.

Nikitich put on his skis and followed the fresh ski tracks, clearly marked in brown-colored snow.

"You son of a bitch, damn jailbird," he swore quietly. "Run away if you wanna. Who cares what happens to you, but why did'ya have to take my rifle? What am I supposed to do here without a rifle? What's wrong with your head? Do y'think I get paid thousands to supply you and your type with rifles? You scoundrel, all you're probably gonna do is throw it away somewhere anyhow. All you can think about is how to get out of the taiga. And you make me sit here with my hands folded and no rifle. You people have no shame, no conscience."

Little by little, it got lighter. It looked like it was going to be overcast and warm. The ski tracks did not go in the direction of the village.

"So you're afraid of people, huh? God damn you . . . the 'Beautiful Life.' You go 'n' take the last ol' rifle from an ol' man. That's OK, it's nothing. But you wo-on't get away from me, my friend. I can best seven of your type, even though you're young!"

The old man was not really angry. He was offended because he'd given shelter to someone who had then up and taken his rifle. Well, didn't that make this guy a bastard?

Nikitich had already gone about three kilometers. It was nearly broad daylight now. You could see the ski tracks far up ahead. "Got up early. Really knew how to do that without making any noise." In one place, the young guy had stopped to smoke. Next to the ski tracks were small holes where the poles had been stuck in. On the snow lay tiny bits of shredded tobacco and a burned out match. "Took my tobacco pouch too!" Nikitich spat out of spite. "A bastard, a real bastard!" He speeded up.

Nikitich spotted the young guy a ways away in a narrow ravine below him. He was moving along at a sensible, even pace. He wasn't hurrying, but moving steadily on. Slung on his back was the rifle.

"Knows how to ski," Nikitich couldn't help observing to himself. He turned off the path and speeded up, going around the young guy, making sure that the top of a long sloping ridge concealed him the whole time. He knew roughly where he'd meet the young guy. He'd come to a narrow clearing. He'd cross it and then go back into the woods . . . and that's where Nikitich would be waiting for him.

"I'll get to see you pretty soon," Nikitich muttered to himself, not without gloating, pushing with all his might on his poles. Strangely enough, he really wanted to see the young guy's handsome face again. There was something intensely attractive about that face. "Maybe it's OK that he's so keen on that beautiful life of his. And when you think about it, what's here for him to do anyway? He'd wither away. Goddamn life, how can you ever understand it all."

At the clearing, Nikitich cautiously peered out from a section of thick growth. No ski tracks there yet. He'd outdistanced him. He darted across the clearing, chose the approximate place where the young guy would emerge, crouched in some bushes, checked to see if his gun was loaded, and waited. Instinctively, with the experienced eye of a hunter, he inspected the rifle. A brand new one from Tula, shiny and smelling strongly of gun oil. "They were going hunting, and they didn't think of how it's bad to have a gun that smells this way. For hunting you also gotta forget about tobacco, and swill your mouth with tea so you don't reek a verst ahead of you, and it's best to put on clothes that have being hanging outside so they don't smell of the house. These hunters make you want to cry."

The young guy came out to the edge of the clearing and stopped. He looked this way and that. He stood for a moment, then crossed the clearing as fast as he could. At that very instance, Nikitich rose to meet him.

"Stop! Hands up!" he commanded loudly, so as to utterly flabbergast the young guy. The latter jerked his head up, and terror showed in his eyes. He was about to raise his hands, but then recognized Nikitich. "You say 'I'm not afraid of anyone,'" said Nikitich, "and you're already shitting in your pants."

The young guy soon recovered from his fright. He smiled his charming smile, though it was somewhat forced.

"Pops. . . . You're playing games . . . like in the movies. Fuck you. I coulda had a heart attack."

"This is what we're gonna do now," Nikitich directed in businesslike fashion. "Don't r'move your rifle, but reach behind with your hands, open it up, and eject the shells from the magazine. And throw out everything that's in your pocket. I had sixteen shots left. Throw 'em all onto the snow and then move over. If you pull anything, I'll shoot. I'm not fooling."

"Got it, old guy. For some reason, I have no desire to pull anything right now."

"You thief, you've got no shame."

"You said yourself I'd be done for without a rifle in the forest."

"And what was *I* supposed to do without it here?"

"This is your home."

"Come on, come on. 'Your home.' What'ya think I have in my home, a factory?"

The young guy scooped the shells out of his pockets. Fourteen, Nikitich counted. Then with his arms he reached behind his back. Biting his lower lip, squinting, he kept a steady eye on the old man. Nikitich didn't take his eyes off the young guy either. In his hands he held the cocked rifle, the barrels level with the young guy's chest.

"What's taking you so long?"

"Can't get them out."

"Pick them out with your fingernails or rap on the stock with your fist."

One shell fell out, then a second.

"Good. Now move over there."

The young guy obeyed. Nikitich picked up the shells and put them in the pocket of his fur jacket. "Toss me the rifle, but don't you move."

The young guy took off the rifle and threw it to the old man. "Now sit down right where you're standing, and we'll have a cigarette. Throw me the pouch too. You also lifted that."

"I gotta smoke."

"That's all you say, 'I gotta this, I gotta that.' You didn't even give me a thought, you tricky devil. What exactly was *I* supposed to smoke?"

The young guy lighted up. "Can I take a little extra for myself?"

"Take some. You got matches?"

"I got some."

The young guy took some of the tobacco for himself and tossed the pouch to the old man. The old man lit up also. They sat about five paces apart.

"Did they leave? Those night guys?"

"They're sleeping. They're good at that. They're not hunting, just fooling around. They want to have a good time, and back in the district it's not easy to get away with that. Everything's in the public eye. So they go somewhere out of sight."

"Who are they?"

"Officials. They waste ammunition for no good reason."

"Hmm . . . yeah."

"Did'ya think I wouldn't catch up with you?"

"I didn't think nothing. You knew one of them. Who is he? Called him by his last name . . . Protokin, was that it?"

"Works in the social security office. I was applying for a pension for my old lady. I saw him there."

The young guy looked inquisitively at the old man.

"Is that the place where they approve trips to health resorts?"

"Un-huh."

"You're fogging something, old fella. D'ya wanna to throw me in prison? On account of the rifle. . . ."

"What the fuck do I need to throw you in prison?" said Nikitich straight out.

"Sell me the rifle, will you? I got money."

"No," Nikitich said firmly. "If you'd asked last night in a nice way, I might've. But since you've played such a dirty trick on me, I won't."

"I couldn't wait 'til they woke up, could I?"

"You should've called me outside during the night. 'This is the way it is, Pops,' you'd say. 'I really don't want to talk with these people. Sell me your rifle,' you'd say. 'I'm gonna leave.' But you up 'n' stole it. In these parts they chop off your hands for stealing."

The young guy put his elbows on his knees and rested his head on his arms. In a muffled voice he said, "Thanks for not giving me away yesterday."

"Anyway, you won't get to your freedom."

The young guy jerked his head up. "Why not?"

"To cross all of Siberia . . . that's no small joke."

"All I have to do is get to the railroad and then I can catch a train. I got IDs. But being here without a rifle is bad news. Sell me yours, OK?"

"No, not even if you beg me."

"I'd be turning over a new leaf. Be good 'n' help me, Pops."

"And just where did you get your IDs? Probably did someone in, didn't you?"

"People can make IDs."

"They're fake. Think they won't catch you with fake IDs?"

"You worry about me like you're my mother. You keep repeating like a parrot, 'They'll catch you, they'll catch you.' I'm telling you *they won't catch me*."

"And where'll you get the dough for all that champay-nee you like to drink . . . if you're gonna do honest work?"

"I jabbered away like a fool yesterday. Pay no attention. I got drunk."

"Aw, you. . . ." The old man spat a caustic yellow glob of saliva onto the snow. "You young people have all the time in the world to live and to live full lives. . . . But you're just like those . . . you're like madmen chasing all over the world, and you can't find yourself a place in it. What gnawing hunger drives you to steal? No, the good life is what makes you so crazy, damn you. You've never really had your ass burned."

"How should I put it, Pops. . . ."

"So who's supposed to be to blame for you?"

"Forget it," the young guy pleaded. "Listen. . . ." He looked anxiously at the old man. "They're waking up right now and they'll see that the rifle's gone. And we're gone. Aren't they gonna come after us?"

"They won't wake up until the sun's out."

"How do you know?"

"I know. They were hung over when they came last night. It's nice 'n' warm in the hut. The heat'll exhaust 'em. It'll make them sleep until dinnertime. They're in no hurry to go anywhere."

"Hmm . . . yeah," muttered the guy sadly. "Things are getting messy."

Snow suddenly began falling in big thick flakes, wet and heavy.

"That's good for you." Nikitich looked upward.

"What is?" The young guy also looked upward.

"The snow. It'll cover all your tracks."

The young guy held out his palm and held it that way a long time. The snowflakes melted on his palm.

"It'll soon be spring," he said with a sigh.

Nikitich looked at him, as if wanting to retain from this last encounter a clear and lasting memory of this man, so uncommon in these parts. He pictured the young guy pushing on through the night, alone and unarmed.

"How are you going to spend your nights?"

"I'll doze by a fire. Won't really get much sleep."

"You people oughta do this running away in the summer. Everything'd be easier."

"They don't let you apply for the best times to run away. It'll be bad news with grub. Between villages your guts'll stick to your back. So . . . OK. Thanks for the hospitality." The young guy got up. "You better go back, 'cause those guys of yours, they're gonna wake up. . . ."

The old man took his time. "You know, there is one way out of this situation," he said slowly. "I'll give you the rifle. Tomorrow around two or three A.M. you'll get to the village where I live. . . ."

"Then what?"

"Don't rush me. You'll get there. You'll go up to some hut on the outskirts. You'll say you found a rifle . . . or . . . no, we should think up something better, so you can leave the rifle there. From our village the road goes straight to the station, twenty versts. Nothing to be afraid of there. Vehicles travel back and forth. You'll be at the station before dawn. You'll come across only one clearing. From it, from that clearing there's another road that goes to the left. Don't take that one. It goes to the district center. Keep on going straight."

"Pops. . . ."

"Wait a minute. What are you goin' to do with the rifle? If you say you found it, they'll get scared and go looking. I'd be really sorry not to have the rifle back. It's a little old, but I wouldn't trade it for three of those." Nikitich pointed at the brand-new rifle.

The young guy looked gratefully at the old man, undoubtedly trying even harder to make the gratefulness in his eyes seem still greater. "Thanks, Pops."

"Hold onto your thanks. How'll I get the rifle back?"

The young guy stood up, went over to the old man, and sat down next to him. "Let's think of some way. I'll hide it somewhere, and you'll get it later."

"Where are you gonna hide it?"

"In a haystack somewhere not far from the village."

Nikitich fell to thinking. "What'll you be able to make out there when it's night? Here's what you do: knock at the hut at the edge of the village, ask where Mazaev, Efim, lives. They'll show you. He's my buddy. You'll go to Efim and you'll say, 'Met up with Nikitich in the taiga. He was taking some 'ologists to Snaky Marsh Plain.' Tell him, 'Used up his shells, and he asked me to bring his rifle to you, so he wouldn't have to drag it around for nothing.' Say I'll be at his place the day after tomorrow, and tell him not to let anybody know that I was taking 'ologists somewhere. 'He'll make some money,' say, 'and then he'll come and you'll have a drink together before his old lady takes it all away from him.' Got it? Leave me enough now for a bottle . . . otherwise Efim will never leave me in peace—and good luck to you. I'm giving you shells . . . six of them. Two more with buckshot . . . just in case. If you don't use them, throw them into the snow near the village out a ways. Don't give them to Efim. He's clever, he'd smell a rat. You got all that?"

"Got it. I'll always remember you for this, Pops."

"Fine. Here's how you get to the village. As soon as the sun comes out—you'll see it the whole way—at first it's gonna be on your left. Even when the sun's higher, keep it on your left. Then near sundown you're gonna turn so that the sun will be to your back, a little to the

VASILY SHUKSHIN

146

right of your head. From there it's a straight shot. Now, let's have a smoke for the road."

They lit up. Somehow, there wasn't anything right then to talk about. They sat a little while, then got up.

"Good-bye, Pops. Thanks."

"Get going."

They were about to take off in different directions, but Nikitich stopped and shouted to the young guy, "Hey! Y'know what, buddy, you had a pretty close shave. That Protokin there is the chief of police. It's a good thing that he didn't wake you up yesterday. Otherwise you wouldn't have outsmarted him. He's a cunning devil."

The young guy looked at the old man and said nothing.

"Right off he'd be asking, 'Where're you from? Where're you headed?' No ID papers in the world would have helped you."

The young guy still said nothing.

"Well, get going." Nikitich slung the unfamiliar rifle onto his shoulder and went back across the clearing, toward the hut. He'd almost got all the way across the clearing when he heard what sounded like the deafening crash of a tree branch right under his ear. At that very moment, in his back and in the back of his head, it seemed as though several fists struck him hard from behind, shoving him forward. He fell face down in the snow—and heard and felt nothing more. He didn't hear someone covering him with snow and saying, "It's better this way, Pops. Safer."

When the sun came out, the young guy was already far from the clearing. He didn't pay attention to the sun.

He went on without looking around, his back to it. He looked ahead. The wet snow whispered in the air. The taiga was waking up. The thick spring smell of the forest was slightly stupefying; it made your head spin.

VLADIMIR MAKANIN

ONE
OLD MAN

And so life goes on. There are bright moments—then
their opposite, more ordinary moments, duller ones.
There are more of these ordinarier moments. They come
one after another, ordinary and routine, a vast age of
them. Then, suddenly, tied to all of this, you detect in
yourself a small change, some new trait.

You're home, say. It's evening. Friends have stopped
by. Someone says something about someone. "A scoundrel," he says about that person. "Just let me tell you
what a scoundrel he is." So he tells you all about it. You
of course listen, and on the spur of the moment you
begin defending the guy. "Maybe he's not a scoundrel,
maybe he did that unintentionally?" "What d'ya mean
unintentionally?" "Well, maybe he wanted to do his best.
He really wanted to, but then the circumstances were
such that. . . ." Words are exchanged and, before you
know it, there's an argument. Eyes light up and on your
faces there's a somewhat odd expression, not a convivial
one. The wife comes in. She wants to know why we're
calling each other shitheads. Don't you care that the children are listening?

The children—now she's got something there. Hard

to deny that, so we lapse into silence. We sit and keep quiet. For a while we don't look at each another. He thinks that he's really been rough on this guy—on me, that is. My anger also subsides. I recall that in actual fact, no matter what story my friend would tell, I'd scoff at him and would touch it up, add something. Maybe this would make his story livelier, but my friend wasn't really interested in sketching things. He didn't want to paint a picture, but to say something about himself, something personal that was painful to talk about. So we both sit, and now, you might say, neither of us stands his ground; like boxers, we break. The conversation is now utterly cordial: about pay, women, Ragulin, Firsov, and Polupanov.

But then a week later we're over at his place. At the friend's. We're sitting, talking about this and that, and I sense that—I can see it in his eyes—he's about to present me with some ready-made notion, something he's prepared in advance. The party's going on, lots of noise all around. He begins by sort of taking me aside or just moving closer at the table we're all sitting around. "By the way, I found a flaw in you," he says. "Yeah?" "Isn't it true that man must reflect the world in its entirety? Well, to some extent. Right?" "I guess so." "But you don't," he says. "I've found a defect in you." "Are you trying to offend me?" "Don't try to joke your way out of it," he says. "In the world, y'know, no matter what you think and do, there's still a prosecutor, judge, and defender. Right?" "Well, maybe." "So there! That means that in every person too it oughta be the same. But in you this triad is missing!"

So, it turns out that I am too much of an advocate; I feel too much sympathy for people. In me the triad's missing. Everyone at the table smirks. So that's what's wrong with him. And he's a *writer*. Tsk, tsk, tsk. They're kidding, of course, but just the same. . . . So I sit there, scratching my head, yeah, y'know, that's exactly what I am. So I act as if I'm thinking of how I'm gonna respond to this. In actual fact, there'll be nothing impromptu or inspired. I'd also thought along these lines earlier myself, y'know, and I'd done my homework. "You're right," I said. "Now we're just sitting around and shooting the breeze, right?" "Right." "The two of us are shooting the breeze, right?" "Right." "So, in shooting the breeze together, aren't we, y'know, also reflecting the world in its entirety? That same triad, right?" "Well . . . OK." "So, when you make someone out to be a wretch, I complement you by defending him. So, together you and I provide the very same triad."

My response made the point, but the friend right then and there figured out a response to my response. Then I, you could say, responded to his response to my response. Scholasticism of the purest sort was in progress. It was like a child placing building blocks one upon another, then another, and another. The company's giving me an inexpressively glum look. That one's the host, so he can be forgiven, but why does the other one, who writes, have to make so much of it? He's a guest just like us, isn't he? Finally everyone was shouting that we should be quiet—our wives that we should shut up. Luckily, at this point, the building blocks collapsed all by themselves.

Or take this. An entirely different experience. At a bus stop I meet a man, unexpectedly. I know him. Actually, it's more than that. At one time, he was my boss and he treated me shamelessly. You don't need to know all the details. What is important is that he rubbed my nose in the dirt, and at the bus stop many years later it's the only thing you remember. We now both emit "hellos" at the same time. We stand there, and you somehow can't part ways because to part ways would be totally illogical and ridiculous—and the bus seems to take forever getting there. I notice that he looks a little frightened. He's remembered of course, and he's a human being like everyone else. He's afraid of me. My impulse is to meet him halfway, to help him. "Summer's a scorcher," I say. "Yeah, the summer is very hot," he says. Then he begins to talk rapidly. Has to arrange for his wife to get accommodations at a resort, he says. Has to arrange for his children as well. I just can't get it done, he says. In telling me this, he's so sad and he frowns so and he seems so utterly dejected because he can't make the arrangements that his objective rings loud and clear. He begins telling me about how his rheumatism bothers him. Then he stops short, falls silent. The rheumatism seems somehow too obviously calculated to elicit my sympathy. Then more talk about the accommodations, those damn accommodations again. Well, he just can't arrange them, and they *are* his wife and children, y'know. . . .

An odd sense of pity gradually comes over me. Not that I'm forgiving him, no Christian virtue at work in me. I'm not going to forgive him and I don't. But there's this pity that keeps sneaking up on me. It's not like I feel sorry for him now, not for him specifically, but for all of us. You see, this is the way we are, it's just the way we are. "I know. Arranging for accommodations at a resort can really be a pain in the ass," I say. "You should also try through the Amalgamated Union." Now, y'know, I say this as if hearing a person beside me say it, and the amazing thing is that doing so pains me and makes me ashamed. My forehead gets damp, my whole body suddenly is in a sweat (his body's already been this way a long while). Finally the bus comes. At long last. That's how it happened.

It's ridiculous, of course, to say that you're not a judge. This is no more than an assertion, and, more important, it's untrue. Not the whole truth. That is, you torment yourself because of your very unjudgelike character trait. You torment yourself over and over, and then as a direct consequence of this torment it's like a weapon emerges (another interpretation: you're not tormenting yourself as much as you are ridding yourself of that torment). For a while you're aggressive. You shout, make assertions, and sometimes you lose your cool, punch somebody. But, y'know, this'll only last for a while, for a short while. Then, y'know, you'll feel uncomfortable, ashamed of yourself. Then you begin to think: maybe my unjudgelike mode was right for me. Doesn't everyone act and speak the way they know best? Whatever's in their power to do. Then you mentally conclude that laughter is the best medicine for you and that you really knew all along. Whatever's not to your liking you should laugh at. Laughing of course hurts, but it never destroys anyone.

So you live, and in a manner of speaking you pretty much know how things could be better and more humane. It's as if you both understand this and keep this in mind, but during both the laughter and the brief aggressiveness you still hear and still sense that same moving, gentle tone. It's like you carry it inside you. By no means a judge, no, not a judge.

It may well be that essentially this is nothing more than a personal impression. I was strongly influenced by a man. He lives in a city I haven't lived in for years. He's sixty (if you're thinking that I'm going to palm off a description of some sort of Christlike character, you're way off base).

This is an evil man; he's not embittered, but just a cold and rancorous old man. Now, old age has played this trick on him. He has his quirks, quirks that correspond to his meanness. For instance, for at least eight years now he has interpreted and explained the *Divine Comedy* to people, or so he claims. These are his very own words. Of course, there's nothing wrong with this and some good may come of it. After all, he kowtowed his whole life, so why not now do what you want? A person is free to choose, isn't he? And he'd chosen to interpret not just anything, but the *Divine Comedy*. Avid reader he wasn't. In fact, before this I'd never once seen him with a book in his hands.

He's glad to explain his main idea: that the sins of our day are different and therefore that punishment needs to be assigned differently. Not quite the way it is in Dante. He talks and explicates categorically. Sometimes he'll settle himself comfortably on a bench, holding the fat folio anniversary edition, beckon someone to listen, and explain the content of the page he's opened to, tapping the binding with a small pencil. Neat and clean, his mien noble, and strict in manner (now right here even I am very tempted to let compassion interfere. After all, this is an old man—and don't we all have old age to look forward to? But let's wait and see before we judge him).

More often than not he'll sit in the sunshine in carefully "guarded" loneliness, sit on a bench—but don't think this is a pose. He'll really be engrossed in his own thoughts. He'll be completely absorbed and suddenly let out loud, cawing sounds, (beginning with a *t* rather than a *c*), "T'Hell! T'Hell! T'Hell!"

This he does with his mouth slightly open, but open in a way that's frightening. He's pondered, weighed someone's transgressions, and now some wretch is falling headlong into an "evil" crevice marked with a number that has just been readied for him. The old man's outcries resound unexpectedly, their sounds blending together. Women hanging out the wash shudder, the horrid drawn-out "t'ell–t'ell–t'ell!" cutting through the entire courtyard.

For all the tenants and neighbors, this is the one and only future path. They're given no choice. He's read *The Inferno*. As he says himself with a very malicious smile, he'll take up the matter of Paradise a little later. So he sits with the sun warming his old bones, and staring straight and hard at passersby with the conceit of a god-prosecutor tapping his pencil. So, the world is being plunged into darkness, and a male neighbor is already burning in hellfire while a female one, poor thing, weighed down by her troubled existence, who loves to complain and bemoan her fate, lies helpless, dashed to the ground with eyes sewn shut (the lot of complainers). He especially likes doling out punishments to his relatives. Any surprise?

But you know, I remember that this old man used to be an entirely different person. He was cheerful. And kind. My first memory of him is from way back when I was a child. The old man was young then, his name Grushkov, Savely Grushkov. On Sunday he would sit on the stoop of his house, dangling his bare legs in the hot dust, and sing

> Oh, no matter what happens, don't be cast down . . .

and peel potatoes, his knife following the beat. It's like a picture out of my childhood.

Now here's another story from those times. Not far away, there was a workshop being built. They didn't allow kids to go onto the building site, and to guard its fascinating nooks and crannies and stairways, they installed a dolt named Senya. After a while any other guard would have become less vigilant. However, this dolt Senya never faltered. He had a motorlike evenness to him. Wouldn't let anyone in even if you were on death's door. An ideal watchman. Finally, one day, displaying brutality he didn't know was in him, he bashed a kid with a piece of board. Of course, this meant that Senya had to quit. Moreover, he was shaking like a leaf because the kid's father and two uncles were big guys. . . . And no one else except Savely Grushkov stood up for Senya in this business.

After a week went by, passions had cooled, yet Senya continued to live with Grushkov, sharing the latter's small quarters. He still looked around fearfully whenever he had to go outside. Then one day, Petya Demin (the very kid Senya whacked) and I went up to the house, and

Grushkov was on the stoop singing

> Oh, no matter what happens, don't be cast down . . .

and peeling potatoes.

Us kids, of course, were feeling sorry for Senya and this is why we'd come. "Fine, come on in. Go and see him," Savely Grushkov told us. We went into his room. Senya was sitting half-naked (at that moment, Grushkov's wife, Auntie Pasha, was washing his things) and was shaking either from the cold or because he was still frightened. We patted him gently on the head, asked him how things were going, left him and went back out to Grushkov.

We hemmed and hawed, stood for a while, then asked, "Uncle Savely, why do they call Senya a dolt? Why do they laugh at him?"

Without interrupting his potato peeling, Grushkov said, "Do you want us to cry over him?"

"Don't you laugh at him sometimes too?" we asked.

"Yeah, I do."

"But isn't it bad to laugh at him?"

"It's bad."

Grushkov continued to peel potatoes. Now he was only whistling the tune of his song. Then, out of the blue, he came up with an explanation. We were struck by what we heard.

"Y'know, if you think about it, this is how he makes his living. He's really a dolt. People laugh at him, and later they feel sorry for him. If they didn't laugh, they wouldn't feel sorry."

"How's that?"

"Here's how. If they didn't know he was a dolt, they wouldn't think twice about beating him up, even killing him. Normal people are beaten up for the things he does, do y'see?"

Grushkov threw a peeled potato in the water with a loud plop and began to laugh. "I might as well teach him to play the accordion. He'll live to be a hundred!"

One more experience. Later on, when I was a university student, I made a trip to see him. On the street, I met Auntie Pasha, Grushkov's wife, who started jabbering right away. "Now, come on, come on" (as though she'd seen me yesterday). "You come to visit. Ain't that great? Come on. Savely will be glad to see you."

On the way, she told me what was new. "Just like in the old days, no one makes Savely bashful. He used to weave baskets, make chairs and toy whistles, but now he's lost his senses completely, the impish old devil!"

"I remember the toy whistles."

"'Member the dishes he used to make out of clay? What for only the devil knows."

"The little pitchers?"

"Yep, those."

I remembered that Savely Grushkov liked any sort of craft work. Daytime at a construction site and evenings at home. He'd plod on all day long. Auntie Pasha was embarrassed to say what the new addition to his creative repertoire was. She just snorted, "Fooey! In the eyes of the neighbors, we're a disgrace and nothing more."

When we got there, the first thing I heard was "Vzzz

. . . vzzz." Sounded like a plane. The sound stopped. Savely greeted me. "Hello, Sinner!" (This was his favorite phrase, although at that time he hadn't begun reading Dante. Hadn't even heard of him.)

Auntie Pasha cooked dinner and set the table. Savely, beaming just like he always did, asked me questions about his son. He had a son and a daughter studying in Moscow. I rarely saw them. But I did see them. So we'd hit upon a topic for conversation right away, one that would last for a long time.

"You see, Moscow's really a hard place to live in," mused Grushkov. "My son wrote me recently, and it's not even a letter, just a glorified note. About this and that. I sense that he can't take the pace of life there." He went on. "Pace of life is no joke. So I sent him a letter back right away. Included a hundred clams. And just imagine. The next letter from him was different. Still short, but quite different. In sync with the pace of life."

His voice took on a dreamlike quality.

"Now picture to yourself my son walking along a street. He's tense. Work's on his mind. Relations with his superiors. No friends. You have to make friends. And you also need food for the soul. You need the love of a woman. You also need to make merry."

"You better be quiet, you old fool," said Auntie Pasha.

"Why should I? You need all this. You really need all of this. And how do you get all that you need? With money of course. If he's going to be late, he'll take a taxi. When his stomach growls, he can go to a restaurant. And going somewhere, he can be happy and think, 'Good ol'

Dad, if you only knew how great things are for me in Moscow!'"

"You don't say. Think he's gonna keep you in mind?" snorted Auntie Pasha (she was now taking offense on her son's behalf: why should he think about things that don't matter much!).

Savely went on, disregarding what she said. "You know yourself how skilled I am with my hands. I've just found myself an odd kind of work."

"Now you be quiet. Shame on you!" Auntie Pasha cut him off.

For some reason, dishes painted with strange patterns came to mind.

Neighbors arrived. They began to talk all at once. This one had a son in Kiev, another in Moscow. That's right, the pace of life was a serious matter. Were "our kids" going to withstand that pace or not? A neighbor came who sang well—and they all began singing. I recall being stuffed and tipsy and turning in on a folding bed that had been made up for me. I fell asleep quickly and easily.

I woke up early. The Grushkovs were already up. Auntie Pasha was washing dishes and cleaning up from the previous evening. Coming from the partly partitioned-off second tiny room of their house was the sound I'd heard before "Vzzzeek . . . vzzzeek." It was clear now that this was a plane. There was also the strong smell of freshly shaved wood. Yawning, wearing only my undershorts, I looked in through the half-opened door. Savely Grushkov was making coffins. That's what they were, coffins. They had such bright and cheery designs on them that I wondered if customers wouldn't reject them one by one. Three stood finished in the corner, and the one in front of Savely was being worked on. Savely stood with his back to me and didn't notice I was there.

"Vzzzeek . . . vzzzeek. . . ."

Auntie Pasha touched me on the elbow. "Don't say nothing to no one 'bout this. OK?"

"OK." (I understood that she meant their children.)

"Or they'll be laughing at him." And then she explained, "In our town it's hard to get these things made. They're renovating the office where you place orders. And Savely often won't even ask to be paid."

"That's foolish. Work is work."

"He thinks so too. But, y'know, it's embarrassing. After all, at work he's a supervisor, sometimes he's called an engineer."

Savely shouted from his room, "What are you whispering about out there? Come 'ere."

"I got plenty to do!" retorted Auntie Pasha and went back to washing dishes.

I went into his room. Savely was just finishing the coffin he was working on. In the corner, I saw the whistles familiar to me from my childhood. Little pitchers. He lit a cigarette. No matter what he did, Savely could not stifle the pride he took in work well done. He was an artist. The feeling of professionalism had gone to his head. He moved a little to the side so as to get the best view of his creation and, looking over the magnificent coffin and inhaling his cigarette with pleasure, said emphatically, "What a beaut!"

But now there's only the cawing "t'ell-t'ell-t'ell!" and

the noble mien and those clean fingers holding the pencil. Nothing else. I've loved this old man a long, long time. And I love him now. When I think of how this same old man used to talk to people—and I'd hear and remember him saying, his eyes aglow with triumph and defiance: "Live it up, Sinner. Be passionate and live it up while you still can. . . . Live it up and don't be afraid of anything!"

LUDMILA PETRUSHEVSKAYA

"WATERLOO

BRIDGE"

By now everyone called her "Grandma" or "Mommy" on
public transport and on the street.

She was forever Granny Olya to her grandchildren,
and her grown-up daughter, a school geography teacher,
heavy and large, was still living with her mother, and the
daughter's husband, a nonentity of a photographer who
worked in some studio (a misalliance that had its origin
in a resort)—this husband sometimes would come home,
but other times wouldn't even show his face.

Granny Olya herself had lived without a husband
for a long, long time. He was always going away on business trips, and then he'd returned—but not home, and
he didn't give a damn about anything, gave it all up:
belongings, suits, footwear, and books about the movies.
Everything was left with Granny Olya, no one knew why.

So the both of them, she and her daughter, sunk into
despair and did nothing to return these things to their
owner. It'd be painful to call somewhere, search out the
person, and, worse still, have to meet him.

Papa obviously didn't even want this himself, and it
was obviously awkward for happy newlyweds, who had
a small son, to have to come for their belongings to an

apartment where his grandchildren and his wife-grand-mother huddled together.

Maybe, thought Granny Olya, *that* wife of his had said, "No need to give a damn about anything. What we need we can buy later on."

Maybe she was well off, unlike Granny Olya, who was used to beet salad and sunflower seed oil, and shoes purchased in an orthopedic shop for needy invalids that looked like children's shoes, with lacings, and they were wider than normal—to allow for growths.

Granny Olya was shabby: meek, with bulging eyes behind spectacles, featherlike hair on a small head, a stout figure, and wide feet.

Granny Olya was, however, an extremely kind soul, forever fussing over someone, dragging herself with bags to every moldy relative, hanging about hospitals, even going to tidy up graves, all by herself.

Her daughter the geography teacher didn't support her mother in these efforts, although she was ready to knock herself out for her so-called girlfriends; she'd feed them, listen to them, but not Granny Olya, not on your life.

To make a long story short, Granny Olya would readily bolt from the house, having prepared a lot of beet salad and fried up a mess of cheap fish, while her daughter the geographer, sedentary like many family types, would urge her girlfriends to come to her place where a wide-ranging discussion of life went on drawn from examples of personal experience.

The geographer's husband was usually absent. This husband from the photo studio habitually led a second existence by the light of a red lamp in the photo lab, where things could go on and no one was the wiser. The geographer-daughter once passed through this red lamp, having returned from the resort in a stupefied state—a youthful, bespectacled, hulking girl with swollen eyes and a mouth that seemed frozen, and then she, the fool, brought the photographer home (moreover, one who was paying alimony and without a place of his own) to her respectable mama and, at that time, papa to live in their small three-room professor's apartment.

But bygones will be bygones. Much water has flowed under the bridge, and Granny Olya, left by herself after the professor's departure without anything, no work experience, no prospects for a pension, and not a kopeck to her name . . . she had to live in the passageway (after the father's departure, the photographer and the geographer quickly took over the separate room, the so-called study; earlier they'd lived in the room beyond the passageway with the children and now they'd spread out to favor family life, while Granny Olya slept on the sofa in the living room as if stuck there). In her new profession, she had to tramp and splash a great deal through puddles—she became an insurance agent—and would knock persistently on the doors of strangers, ask to be let in, and fill out insurance policies in kitchens. She always carried a plump briefcase, she—a kind person with a sweaty nose and the craw of a mother goose.

Plain, garrulous, devoted, eliciting the complete trust and friendly disposition of strangers (but not of her own daughter, who didn't give a damn about her mother and felt her papa's departure was fully justified), such was

Granny Olya, and she didn't live for herself at all, but filled her head with other people's affairs, and in the very process of getting acquainted would tell her own story: how she'd been a magnificent conservatory singer, who had married and gone with her husband on assignment to a national preserve in the boondocks, how he'd done his dissertation there and she'd had a child, etc., in proof of which Granny Olya would even execute a phrase from the romance "Tenderly and Languidly I Long for You," laughing boisterously with her amazed listeners at the unexpected effect she had of making the tumblers in the sideboard start to ring and of frightening pigeons on the windowsill into flight.

Understandably, that daughter of hers and even her grandchildren could not endure Grandma's singing, since at the conservatory they'd made an opera and not a drawing-room singer out of Granny Olya—what's more, a dramatic soprano of uncommon timbre.

However, everybody has their weak moments, and as for Granny Olya, one day she just couldn't withstand the burden and trouble and futility of ringing the doorbells of strangers, and suddenly found herself at a movie theater—solely for her own enjoyment. It was warm there; there was a snack bar, a foreign film, and, what was interesting, a large number of women her own age by the entrance, just like her—with their handbags.

It was as if some witches' Sabbath was going on by the doors of the small movie theater, and, drawn by strange feelings and going against her conscience and persuading herself she would only rest a little while,

Granny Olya marched to the ticket window, bought herself a ticket, and entered the alien warmth of the foyer.

At the snack bar people clustered. There were even young people, couples. Granny Olya also got herself some sort of questionable sweet ade, a sandwich, and what was supposedly a pastry—all for a fantastic sum. If you're going to enjoy yourself, why not do it right? Then she wiped her lips with her husband's checked handkerchief and, agitated for reasons she could not comprehend, went into the hall along with the crowd, sat down, removed her winter hat secured with a rubber band and her scarf, unbuttoned her threadbare coat, once stylish—after all, it was blue gabardine and silver fox—but best now not to look in the mirror. Then the lights dimmed and up came heaven.

On the screen Granny Olya saw all of her dreams: herself, very young, slender, like one of the reeds in the national preserve, with a bright face, and also her husband, as he should have been, and that life she for some reason had not lived.

Life was full of love, the heroine was dying, just as we all will die, in poverty and illness, but en route there was a candlelight waltz.

At the end, Granny Olya cried, and everyone around her blew their noses, and then, moving her feet very slowly, Granny Olya set out anew like a industrious bee to collect premiums, again ran up against two locked doors, and, defeated in her professional pursuits, crawled home.

The bus with tearing windows, the steamy subway,

the last few blocks on foot, the climb to the third story of the building, the thick domestic aroma, the voices of small children in the kitchen, her own, beloved, familiar . . . stop!

Suddenly Granny Olya saw before her, as in a dream, full of tenderness and concern, the face of Robert Taylor.

The next day, as early as possible in the morning, she again rushed to that part of the city, found customers at home, and collected money from them; in addition, she struck up several acquaintances in the kitchens of these customers' communal apartments, telling them the advantages of insuring their lives and how in the process to boot they would receive, like a prize, compensation for all injuries, fractures, and operations—the most enticing part—and the people listened to her willingly, became pensive about fate, and so her business moved forward. Then Granny Olya rushed headlong to the familiar movie theater for the morning show.

Another film was already playing there, however, a children's film.

Nonetheless, at the ticket window Granny Olya found one half-familiar face, that of a still rather young grandma from yesterday in a tall astrakhan hat, who also had flown to this movie theater as early as possible in the morning, and now, deprived, was asking where the poster announcing the movie was, obviously so that she could make her way to the other movie house where her favorite picture was playing.

Granny Olya pricked up her ears, asked the same question, understood the crux of the problem, and the next day—but only the next day—all by her lonesome, minced her way to a rendezvous with her beloved, returning once more to that enchanting world of her other life.

Now she already felt less shy in the midst of the other grandmas, and less ashamed of herself as well, and when she left the theater she saw happy, tearstained faces, and found herself wiping away tears with a large men's handkerchief left to her as a memento, like the men's woolen underwear, so-called huntsmen's underwear, which she put on when the weather was extremely cold, and the drawers which she wore at night, while her daughter wore to school her papa's checked shirts under a sarafan. You had to take life as it comes!

"Good heavens," thought our honest Granny Olya whose heart was pure as gold. "What's the matter with me? I must be bewitched. Worst of all, these old women are running from one movie theater to another. It's awful."

She did not think of herself as an old woman; anyway, she still had a lot ahead of her. They valued Granny Olya at work, her customers respected her, she supported the family now, and had even bought the children an aquarium and gone with them to the Bird Market for tropical fish, hoping to forget *that* which was the Main Thing. (Granny Olya knew how to govern her passions; she knew how to sacrifice herself, as she had in the boondocks, for example.)

However, her understanding of the situation wasn't helping her a bit, as Granny Olya admitted to herself after a routine visit to customers in their apartments. No matter what they spoke about, she kept returning again and again to her favorite name, Robert, to the name of the film—"Waterloo Bridge"—and to details from the lives of its actors and actresses. People attempted to tell her about their own lives, and Granny Olya again mentioned, say, the picture show she had been to the day before yesterday and at what movie theater the film was still playing.

She did sense now that she was sliding downward somewhere, especially in the eyes of her customers, that she no longer listened so assiduously to all their tales, no longer grew interested as before in discussing their communal apartment intrigues, judgments, betrayals, plans; she found herself now listening to all this absentmindedly, nodding and sniffing as she looked for her handkerchief, while through all this rubbish, scum, and flotsam of life there appeared before her *that,* the *Main Thing: his torments.* And, in passing, *her* torments as well.

And finally, Granny Olya found her place in life once and for all.

She cast aside all conventions. No longer did she consider insurance and collecting premiums to be her most important task; rather it was inspiring customers who were submerged in the dust of the earth, inspiring them with the thought that there exists another life, another, unearthly, higher one, of picture shows, say, at 7 and 9 P.M., at the Screen of Life cinema on Sadovo-Karetny Street.

And as she expounded this, her eyes shone through her thick glasses.

What the reason for this was, why she was doing this, Granny Olya did not know herself, but she knew that she had to bring people happiness, new happiness. She had to recruit more and more supporters of "Robbie," and she experienced toward her rare recruits (male and female alike) a mother's tenderness—but, on the other hand, also a mother's strictness, for she was their guide in that world, and she guarded its rules and traditions against their incursions. She soon had a fat notebook with hand-copied newspaper articles about Robert Taylor and Vivien Leigh. In it were pasted their portraits and stills from the movie. Her good-for-nothing son-in-law had actually done some work for her under a red lamp in his dubious photo lab: even one tuft of wool from a mangy sheep is a plus!

It wasn't good that hordes of little ladies and grannies congregated to perform rites, which had already become like some Sodom and Gomorrah, with sobbing, hysterics, and poems passing from hand to hand. "Robbie's" birthday was established, and this nativity of his was observed in the foyers of movie theaters, where they drank Cahors red wine and vodka and were noisy before the show, but Granny Olya, as the strict high priestess, celebrated all by herself at home in her kitchen.

Meeting one another, they would tell how it *had been*. Granny Olya, however, didn't let this nonsense of theirs affect her. She kept her secret, but in the soft of the night wrote poetry, and then, unable to resist temptation herself, chose the right moment and imparted it to her customers. Of course, she never thought of reciting it to the little grandmas, for, if she did so, they in retaliation immediately read back homegrown stupidities like, "And many girls he caressed so sweetly." Nah!

Granny Olya would mutter her exalted poetry to select female customers hurriedly, sniffling, her glasses dimmed by tears. Her listeners would suffer her, glancing aside, the way they did when she, feeling deeply moved, sang with all her might. Granny Olya did fully grasp the awkwardness of her situation, but just couldn't help herself.

Where, when, and how you are enslaved by passion, you fail to notice and, as a result, you fail to exercise self-control or sound judgment, to consider the consequences of your actions, but instead, joyfully surrender yourself and eventually find your own path, no matter what that path is. "It doesn't cause any harm," Granny Olya would reiterate to herself as she fell asleep in a happy mood. "I'm an intelligent woman, and this is of no concern to anyone. In the end, it's solely my affair."

And she would drift into a dream about Robert Taylor. Once she even went for a drive with him in an open car, both of them sitting in the backseat with no one else in the landau, not even a chauffeur, and *he* half-embraced Granny Olya's shoulders and sat, devotedly, next to her. Now how can you tell that to anyone?

Only once was there a shameful moment, because you don't just gad about at night—as her daughter the geographer used to say.

Granny Olya was walking with a light step after the movies, somewhere far away, on the outskirts of the city, nearly at the Ilich Gate—desire can be worse than slavery—when a young man, tall and heavy, in a winter hat with the earflaps hanging down, overtook her. (Granny Olya was walking in spritely fashion, her hat perched on one side of her head, and she was singing faintly into the frost, singing to herself the romance "I Opened the

Window.") And this young man, after catching up with Granny Olya, remarked, "What small feet you have!"

"Wha-at?" gasped Granny Olya.

He halted and demanded to know, "What size is your foot?"

"Thirty-nine," answered Granny Olya, amazed.

"That's small," responded the young man sadly, at which point Granny Olya darted past him. Gotta get home, gotta get home. And she ran to the trolley, her briefcase banging.

But later, during the night, when she thought sensibly about it, the sorry sight of the sick young man, shuffling along on the soles of his feet, his unshaven, neglected look, and, what's more, his dark mustache disturbed Granny Olya. Who was he?

She tried to formulate a profile of him based on tried-and-true life stories: his mother had died, he'd had a nervous breakdown, left his job, his sister and family didn't take care of him and chased him out, and so on, but somehow it didn't fit in this instance.

The following day, despite her daughter's warning shrieks, Granny Olya again traveled to the same place where the film was playing, for the same show.

And, having seen Taylor one more time, she began to comprehend who had met her on the dark street after the movie, who it was that walked along sick and neglected, miserable, unshaven but with a mustache. And, you know, if you think about it, who else could have dragged himself out to seek his beloved when the whole world had forgotten about her? Who else could be wandering around such a place as the Ilich Gate in 1954, a poor and

sick specter in an undersized coat, abandoned by everyone? He wandered in order to appear on Waterloo Bridge
before that very last soul who had been forgotten by
everyone, abandoned, used like a rag or doormat, and,
what's more, who was literally in the last days of life, on
the verge of leaving it. . . .

TATYANA TOLSTAYA

MY DEAR
SHURA

The first time Alexandra Ernestovna walked past me early
in the morning, she was bathed entirely in pink Moscow
sunlight. Sagging stockings, legs bowed, a black suit,
grease-stained and threadbare. But to make up for it—a
hat! The four seasons of the year—snowballs, lilies of the
valley, cherries, barberries—woven into a wreath on a
pale straw platter attached to the remains of her hair with
a horrendous pin. The cherries had become slightly loose
and knocked together the way wood does. She's ninety, I
thought. But I was off by six years. The sunny air runs
down along the beam from the roof of the cool, old-fashioned house and then again up, up to where you rarely
look, where an iron balcony hangs at an uninhabitable
height, where there's a steep roof, a delicate grating raised
directly against the morning sky, a turret fading away, a
spire, doves, angels—no, I'm not seeing well. Smiling
blissfully, with eyes that had become misty from happiness, Alexandra Ernestovna moves along the sunny side
of the street, moving her prerevolutionary legs in wide,
compasslike fashion. Cream, a bun, and a carrot in a
string bag weigh down her arm and rub on her black,
heavy hem. The wind on legs of its own has come out of

the south, wafting sea and roses, and promising the way up light stairways to heavenly blue lands. Alexandra Ernestovna smiles at the morning, smiles at me. Her black garb, bright hat, rattling with dead fruit, disappears around a corner.

Later on I would run into her on the scorching boulevard. Wilting from the heat, she'd be cajoling a sweaty, solitary child who'd gotten stuck in the over-baked city; she's never had children of her own. A horrid piece of underwear hangs down from under her soiled black skirt. Someone else's child has trustingly dumped its sandy treasures onto Alexandra Ernestovna's lap. Don't get auntie's clothes dirty. That's OK. . . . Let it be.

I used to meet her also in the stuffy air of a movie theater. (Take your hat off, grandma! Can't see a thing!) Alexandra Ernestovna would breath noisily, out of sync with the passions on the screen. She would crinkle the crumpled tinfoil of her chocolate, gluing together her fragile, prescription dentures with a sticky sweet chocolate clay.

In the end, twisting and turning amid a stream of fire-spitting cars at Nikitin Gate and beginning to rush about, she lost her sense of direction, grabbed my arm, and sailed over to a safe shore, having lost forever the respect of the black diplomat hiding behind the green glass of his shiny, low-slung automobile and of his cute curly-haired kids. The black man roared, let out a puff of blue smoke, and sped off in the direction of the Conservatory, and Alexandra Ernestovna, shaking, frightened, goggled-eyed, hung onto me and dragged me to her communal refuge of knickknacks, oval frames, and dried flowers, leaving in her wake a trail of vasodilatin.

Two tiny rooms, a high, molded ceiling. On the peeling wallpaper, smiles, ponders, teases a ravishing beauty—the image of dear Shura, Alexandra Ernestovna. Yes, yes, that's me! In a hat and without the hat and with my hair let down. Oh, so beautiful. . . . And this is her second husband, now that's the third—not a very good choice. Well, why talk about that now. . . . Now, maybe, if she'd made up her mind then to run off to Ivan Nikolaevich? Who is this Ivan Nikolaevich? He's not here. He's being squeezed in an album, stuck into the four precut corners, slammed down by a lady in a bustle, crushed by some sort of short-lived white dogs who died even before the Russo-Japanese War.

Sit down, sit down, what can I get you? Come and see me, of course, for goodness sake, come and see me! Alexandra Ernestovna is alone in the world, so she is always eager to chat.

Fall. Rainy days. Alexandra Ernestovna, do you recognize me? It's me! You remember . . . well, it doesn't matter, I came to visit you. For a visit, oh, my lucky day! Come in, come in, I'll tidy things up. This is how I live— all alone. I've outlived everyone. Three husbands, did you know? And also Ivan Nikolaevich, he wanted me to come, but. . . . Maybe I should have made up my mind to go? What a long life I've had. Now that's me. That's also me. And this is my second husband. I had three husbands, did y'know? To be sure, the third wasn't very. . . .

As for the first, he was a lawyer. A famous one. We

were very well off. In spring we went to Finland, in the summer to the Crimea. White fruitcakes, black coffee. Hats with lace. Oysters—very expensive. In the evening, the theater. So many admirers! He perished in 1919—murdered in the gateway to a building.

Oh, of course, she had affair after affair, how could it have been otherwise? A woman's heart can't offer resistance! Why, just three years ago, a violinist rented a nook from Alexandra Ernestovna. Twenty-six, had won prizes, what eyes he had! Of course, he concealed his love for her in the depths of his heart, but his look gave him away. In the evening Alexandra Ernestovna would ask him, "Some tea?" and he, well, would just look and say no-o-othing! So, do you understand? Cra-a-afty! He kept silent while he stayed with Alexandra Ernestovna, but it was obvious that he was burning from tip to toe, his soul throbbing with passion. Evenings found the two of them together in two small, cramped rooms. Y'know there was something tangible in the air—it was clear to them both. He wouldn't be able to stand it, and would leave. Go outside. He'd wander somewhere till late in the night. Alexandra Ernestovna restrained herself resolutely, giving him no hope. Then it was he who, out of grief, married some woman—no one special. He moved. And once after he got married he ran into Alexandra Ernestovna on the street and gave her his special look. Reduced her to ashes! But again, he said nothing. Buried it all inside him.

To be sure, Alexandra Ernestovna's heart was never empty. Three husbands, by the way. Lived with the second up to the war in a huge apartment. A well-known physician. Famous guests. Flowers. Always merrymaking going on. He died in a merry way too, for when it became clear that his time had come, Alexandra Ernestovna decided to call in Gypsies. Now, don't you think, when things are beautiful, loud, and merry, it's easier to die, isn't it? She couldn't find real Gypsies. But Alexandra Ernestovna—she's inventive—didn't need to think twice. She hired some swarthy guys, and girls too, dressed them up in rustling, glittery, fluttery costumes, flung open the doors to the dying man's bedroom, and they started to jingle, to yell, to sing in a whine. They danced in circles, jumping up and down and squatting: pink, gold, gold, pink! Her husband wasn't expecting this. He'd already directed his eyes to the *other world,* and then suddenly people burst in, twirling shawls, screaming. He sat up, waved his arms and wheezed, "Go away!" But their dancing became more and more lively; they even stomped. So he died. May the Kingdom of Heaven be his. But the third husband wasn't very. . . .

But Ivan Nikolaevich. . . . Oh, Ivan Nikolaevich. There'd only been so much: the Crimea, 1913, striped sunlight coming through a Venetian blind cuts the well-scrubbed white floor into little blocks. Sixty years has passed, and yet. . . . Ivan Nikolaevich simply lost his head. I should leave my husband right away and join him in the Crimea. Forever. She'd promised. Then in Moscow she had thought more about it. Just what was there to live on? And where were they supposed to live? But he deluged her with letters: "My Dear Shura, come to me, come to me!" Here her husband had his own things to do, was rarely home, and there, in the Crimea, on smooth sand under blue skies, Ivan Nikolaevich ran around like a tiger.

"My Dear Shura, it'll be forever!" He himself, poor thing, didn't even have enough money for a ticket to Moscow. Letters and more letters, every day letters for a whole year. Alexandra Ernestovna is going to show them to me.

Oh, how he loved her. To go or not to go?

Human life has four seasons: Spring!!! Summer. Fall . . . Winter? But even winter has passed for Alexandra Ernestovna. Where is she now? Where are her rheumy, colorless eyes directed? Head back and pulling down a red lid, Alexandra Ernestovna puts yellow drops in her eye. Her head is like a small pink balloon seen through the delicate gossamer of her hair. Sixty years ago, did this thin wispy, mouselike tail cloak her shoulders like the black fantail of a peacock? In these very eyes had the insistent but penniless Ivan Nikolaevich been lost once and for all? Alexandra Ernestovna groans and feels for her slippers with gnarled feet.

"Now we're going to drink tea. I won't let you leave without tea. No-no-no. Don't even think about leaving before that."

I really wasn't going anywhere. The very reason I'd come was to have tea. I'd even brought some pastries. I'll put the kettle on, don't trouble yourself. And meanwhile, she'll get out the velvet album and the old letters.

It's a long way to the kitchen, to another city, along an endless, shining floor, polished so heavily that traces of the red polish sticks on your soles for two days. At the end of the hallway tunnel, like firelight in a thick forest of highwaymen, glows a speck, the kitchen window. Twenty-three neighbors make no noise behind their clean white doors. At the halfway point there's a wall phone. A note, pinned up in the past by Alexandra Ernestovna, shows white: "Fire—01. Ambulance—03. In case of my death, call Elizabeth Osipovna." Elizabeth Osipovna herself long ago departed this world. So what? Alexandra Ernestovna forgot.

In the kitchen there's a morbid, lifeless cleanliness. On one of the ranges, someone's cabbage soup is talking to itself. In the corner, there remains still a curly cone of odor where a neighbor smoked a Belomor cigarette. A chicken in a string bag hangs outside the window, as if being punished, dangling in the black wind of the night. A naked wet tree has drooped out of grief. A drunk unbuttons his coat, leaning his forehead against a fence. The sad set modifiers of place, time, and means. And what if Alexandra Ernestovna had agreed then to give up everything and flee south to be with Ivan Nikolaevich? Where would she be now? She had already sent a telegram (AM COMING stop MEET ME stop), packed her things, hidden the ticket as best she could—in the secret compartment of her purse—pinned her peacock-like hair up high, and sat down in the armchair facing the window—to wait. And far away in the south Ivan Nikolaevich, thrown into a tizzy, not believing his luck, rushed to the railroad station—to run about, to worry, to get worked up, to give orders, to hire, to arrange things, to go crazy, to stare at the horizon overcast with sultry haze. And then? She waited in the armchair until evening, till the first bright stars appeared. And then? She pulled the hairpins out of her hair, shook her head. And then? Well, why more "thens"? Life went by, *that's* what happened "then."

The teakettle came to a boil. I'll brew it really strong. An uncomplicated little tune plays on the tea xylophone: lid-let, lid-let, spoon-let, lid-let, potholder, lid-let, potholder, potholder, spoon-let, handle-let, handle-let. Long is the trip back down the dark hallway with teapot and kettle in hand. Twenty-three neighbors listen closely behind their white doors. Is she going to let her wretched tea drop onto our clean floor? I haven't dropped any, don't get excited. With my foot I open the Gothic panels of her door. I've been gone an eternity, but Alexandra Ernestovna still remembers me.

She has gotten out the cracked raspberry teacups, decorated the table with some doilies, and now rummages around the dark coffin of the sideboard, stirring up the bready, biscuity smell that creeps out from behind its wooden cheeks. Don't creep out, smell! I'll catch it and squeeze it back behind the faceted glass doors. There, stay put under lock and key.

Alexandra Ernestovna will get out *marvelous* jam. It'd been given to her. Just try it. No, no, try it. Too good for words. O-o-ooh. Yes, it's something out of the ordinary. Wonderful, isn't it? That certainly is true. Never had anything like this as long as I've lived. Well, I'm so glad, I knew you'd like it. Have some more. Take some, take some, I beg you. (Goddamn, I'm going to have another toothache!)

I like you, Alexandra Ernestovna, I like you very much, especially there in that photograph where your face has such a nice oval quality, and in this one where you've thrown back your head and are laughing and displaying your wonderful teeth, and in this one where you're pretending to be whimsical and you've tossed your hand somewhere to the back of your head so that the fancy lace of your sleeve purposely falls back from your elbow. I like that fast-paced life of yours wherever it happened, though no longer of interest to anyone, your youth which vanished so quickly; your admirers, husbands, now reduced to dust who proceed in solemn succession, all of them, all of them, the ones who called to you and the ones you called to, each one who has passed by and disappeared behind the high mountain of eternity. I'll come visit you, and I'll bring you cream too, and carrots, very good for the eyes, and you'll be so good as to open the long unaired brown velvet albums. Let the pretty high-school girls get some air, let the gentlemen with mustaches limber up, let the gallant Ivan Nikolaevich smile. Never mind, never mind, he can't see you. Don't be embarrassed, Alexandra Ernestovna. . . . You should've decided then. You should have. But she'd already decided. There he is—next to you—just stretch out your hand! Here, take him in your hands, hold him, there he is, flat, cold, glossy, with a gold edge, a slightly yellowed Ivan Nikolaevich. Hey, did you hear that, she's decided, *yes,* she's coming, go meet her, this is it, she's stopped hesitating, go meet her, where are you? Hello!

Thousands of years, thousands of days, thousands of transparent, impenetrable curtains have fallen from the heavens, thickened, formed solid walls, blocked roads, and kept Alexandra Ernestovna from going to her lover lost in the eons. He remains there, on the other side of the years, alone, at a dusty southern station, wandering about the platform covered with spit-out shells of sunflower seeds. He looks at his watch, with the toe of his boot kicks off dusty corncobs gnawed bare, impatiently tearing off small blue-gray cypress cones. He waits and waits and waits for the locomotive to come out of the hot morning distance. She's not coming. She's not going to come. She's deceived him. But, no, no, she really wanted to. She was ready, her bags were packed. White semitransparent dresses had tucked up their knees in the cramped darkness of her trunk, the vanity case squeaks its leather, flashes its silver a bit. The shameless bathing suits barely covering the knees—the arms bare to the shoulder—await their hour, squinting, anticipating. . . . In the hat box, an impossible, ravishing, weightless—oh, words do not suffice—a white zephyr, wonder of wonders! On the very bottom, lying on its back with paws up, sleeps a small case: hairpins, combs, silk laces, fine diamond sand pasted onto emery boards—files for delicate nails, small trifles. A jasmine genie sealed up in a crystal perfume bottle—oh, how it will radiate with a billion rainbows in the blinding light of the sea! She's ready, what got in her way? What always gets in our way? Hurry up, now. Time's passing. Time's passing, and the invisible layers of years get thicker and thicker. The rails rust and the roads become overgrown and the tall weeds grow ever more luxuriant in the ravines. Time flows on, rocking the boat of dear Shura on its back and lapping wrinkles onto her incomparable face.

"More tea?"

After the war, we returned, my third husband and I, right here, to these tiny rooms. My third husband did nothing but whine. The hallway was too long, there wasn't enough light, the windows faced the back. Everything was over for us. The well-dressed guests had died, the flowers had dried up. Rain pounded the windowpanes. He whined and whined—and died, and when and of what—Alexandra Ernestovna didn't really take notice.

She would get Ivan Nikolaevich out of the album, look at him for a long while. How he'd begged her to come! She'd even gone and bought a ticket. Here it is: the ticket. On thick cardboard, numbers in black. If you want to, look at it this way, if you want to, turn it upside down. It's all the same: forgotten symbols of an unknown alphabet, a coded pass there, to that shore.

Perhaps if you figure out what the magic word is, if you guess, if you sit and think hard, or look somewhere, there must be a door, a crack, an unnoticed crooked passageway back there to that day. They've closed everything up. Well, but what if they were careless and left a little crack open? Maybe in some old house, isn't it possible? In the attic, if you pull up some boards . . . or in a dark alley, in a brick wall, a crevice, sloppily filled with brick, hurriedly plastered over, covered with crisscrossed boards in rough-and-ready fashion. Maybe if not here, then in another city. . . . Maybe somewhere in a tangle of rails on a siding stands a passenger car, old and rusted, with a floor that has given way, the very passenger car that dear Shura never boarded?

"Here's my compartment. Excuse me, I need to get through. Please look at my ticket. Here. Everything's on it." Over there, at the other end, are rusty coils from the wheel springs, the rusty red, bent support frames of the walls. In the ceiling blue sky, grass underfoot. That's her rightful seat, hers alone. No one ever occupied it, simply wouldn't have been legal.

More tea? A snowstorm.

More tea? Apple trees in bloom. Dandelions. Lilac. Goodness, how hot it is. Leave Moscow—go to the seashore. See you, Alexandra Ernestovna. I'll tell you what's there, at that end of the Earth. Whether the sea has dried up, whether the Crimea has floated away like a small dry leaf, whether the blue sky has faded. Whether your exhausted, agitated lover has left his voluntary post at the train station.

In the stony hell of Moscow, Alexandra Ernestovna waits for me. No, no, everything is as she told me, everything is as it's supposed to be. There, in the Crimea, invisible but restless in his white tunic, Ivan Nikolaevich paces up and down the dusty platform, digging his watch out of his watch pocket, wiping his shaven neck. Worried, at a loss, he moves back and forth along the dwarfish, latticework fence, rubbing off its fine white powder. Through him, oblivious to his presence, pass pretty, large-featured girls in pants, hippie-looking boys with rolled-up sleeves, wrapped in impudent transistorized baba-ba-bebop; older women in white kerchiefs, with buckets of plums, southern ladies with plastic acanthus clip-on earrings; frail old men in crease-proof synthetic hats. They are passing through, right through, across Ivan Nikolaevich, but he doesn't know, notices nothing, he's waiting, time has strayed from its path, got stuck halfway, somewhere near Kursk, has stumbled over nightingale streams, in its blindness got lost on sunflower plains.

Ivan Nikolaevich, please wait! I'll tell her, I'll let her know. Don't leave, she'll arrive, she really *will,* she's already made up her mind, she's agreed. Keep standing there until . . . nothing to worry about. She'll be there soon. All her things are ready and packed . . . they only need to be picked up. And the ticket's been bought, I know, I swear to you, I saw it—in a velvet album, tucked behind a photograph. It's gotten a little worn, to be sure, but that doesn't matter. I think they'll let her on. There's a problem there for sure . . . she can't get through. Something or other's in the way, I don't remember what. One way or another she'll manage. She has the ticket, doesn't she? That's really important, the ticket. And y'know, the main thing is that she's made up her mind. I'm telling you it's for sure, it's for sure!

You ring five times for Alexandra Ernestovna, the third button from the top. There's a breeze on the landing, the sashes of the dusty stained-glass windows on the stairway have been opened slightly. They're ornamented with frivolous lotus blooms, the flowers of oblivion.

"Who? She passed away."

"How can that be? . . . Just a minute . . . How could that be? But just a little while ago I. . . . Look, I just left there and came back! What are you saying?"

Hot white air rushes at those emerging from the crypt of the entrance, striving to penetrate the eyes. Let me think . . . . They probably haven't picked up the garbage yet, have they? Around the corner on a patch of asphalt stand the trash cans where the spirals of earthly existence mark their end. And just where did you think that is? Beyond the clouds, maybe? Here they are, these spirals, sticking out like the springs of a gaping rotten sofa. Here's where they've dumped everything. The oval portrait of dear Shura, glass broken, the eyes poked out. The pitiful odds and ends of an old woman. Some stockings. . . . The hat with the four seasons of the year. You couldn't use some chipped wooden cherries, could you? Why not? The pitcher with the spout broken off. The velvet album, they stole, of course. Velvet's good for cleaning boots. You're a bunch of fools, I'm not weeping, why should I? The garbage has steamed in the sun. A black bananalike slime has spread over it. The bundle of letters has been trampled down into the muck. "My Dear Shura, now when will you . . . ?" "My Dear Shura, just say the word. . . ." And one letter, which has dried out, circles like a yellow, line-covered butterfly under a dusty poplar, not knowing where to land.

What can I do about all this? Turn around and leave. It's hot. Wind raises the dust. And Alexandra Ernestovna, dear Shura, real as a mirage, crowned with wooden fruit and cardboard flowers, floats smiling along the wavering alley, around the corner, to the south, to the unthinkably distant shining south, to the forsaken platform. She floats, melts, and dissolves into the hot midday.

ANATOLY KIM

DOUBLE
STAR

THE GARRET DWELLER

The garret dweller had returned to a bygone sequence in the orbit of his existence. He'd been twenty then, now he was forty. Out the window of the attic cubbyhole, he sees the branch of a tree drawn by the Creator with faultless perfection. He sees part of the iron roof nearby—red lead paint, brown and dust-covered, and at the corner of the roof the downspout funnel of gray galvanized iron. He sees the dingy yellow building opposite him over which the bare April tree branches cast a pattern, and beyond the branches mysterious windows with frames painted in the same prosaic red lead. Beyond these windows' aspic-like panes, flaccidly hanging tulle curtains languish, not so much as stirring. The lower corner of one window at the very top of the building is occupied by a stack of old papers, piled up haphazardly. To the erstwhile garret dweller, these papers seem to hide someone's hopeless expectations of being able to refashion the entire world or to record instructions about how one can learn to fly by dint of will alone.

The noise of traffic and machinery, like an element of

nature, embraces the world beyond his window, and amid this roar, like odd splashes of primeval life accidentally spared, sound sparrows' cries and the old-mannish cawing of crows. Tiny April snowflakes dance beyond the glass of the small garret window, barely visible, tiny buglike snowflakes, the last feeble offspring of dying winter's cold, and with his eyes—and with endless pity—the garret dweller follows each tiny snowflake's eddy, because all that he sees, he thinks, is nothing but a visual demonstration of the law of irreplaceable loss quietly being proved in real life.

As they were twenty years ago, so now are this garret and the yellow building opposite it and the semi-well of the walled-in courtyard and the clear space to the left of the yellow building's edge and, in the distance, the continuous line of Moscow roofs—that peculiar world populated by cats, puddles, sooty chimneys, and TV antennas. Twenty years ago, the garret dweller, then a third-year university student, going up to the window in the evening, would always see one and the same picture. In the yellow building on the second floor was housed a workshop that produced cardboard items, or some operation that had to do with the manufacture of paper office supplies. A blond woman in a dark blue smock worked at a table with stacks of papers, and in that window she alone was visible, all lighted up by a powerful electrical radiance. There were no other workers nearby, and it was as if she were performing some enchanted task. Spellbound, the young garret dweller viewed her light, most likely chemically bleached hair, and waved to her, and she waved back, the sleeves of her smock rolled up

above the elbow. The student then drew the small window curtain, for he would have to change his clothes, or
have supper, or read his books, but, doing these things,
the young garret dweller would glance again and again at
the white, long-unwashed curtain beyond which hid
enormous nighttime Moscow, its machinery roaring and
clanging, with its thousand constellations of electric
lights—in its great deed poised high above good and evil.

In those years, the youth, living alone in the garret
on K———— Lane, often thought about what causes man
to be in the peculiar situation of having to choose
between good and evil. He wants the former, yet for some
reason chooses the latter. And the great city, like a huge
amoeba, absorbs all people no matter what their choices
and decisions may be, it absorbs and digests them. And
into the sky flies intense smoke from tall chimneys, making you think that clouds are born this way. . . .

So as not to be distracted and mired down in futile
dreams, the student, returning to his room after classes,
would not always part the curtains and look out the window. But several days passed and the garret dweller,
pressing his forehead to the cold pane, again waved, and
the worker girl cheerfully responded with the same sign
of greeting. At heart, the garret dweller was a very con-
ceited person. Now, some twenty years later, he could
speak about this truthfully, but in that year—in the
spring—fighting every evening against the temptation to
part the curtains at his window, he did not think that
pride was what tormented him, but that reason had the
upper hand. He had to study diligently, so that the elec-
tronics industry would gain in his person a fine special-

ist, and here some bleached blond was waving to him, distracting him from his textbooks.

The student had shut and opened the curtains at his window many times, and then one day, at midnight, he found himself standing at the entrance of some business, waiting for the one who'd figured out how to communicate to him the time she'd be done with work by writing on a piece of cardboard the number 12 in big figures. With extreme naïveté and of her own accord, she went to his room and stayed with him. He was agitated, fear-stricken. What if his landlady, straight-laced in these matters, had noticed? Moreover, she was only his second, and he'd never before seen feminine beauty so faultless.

It was not long before he began to visit her often in her strange little room. There wasn't a single square corner in it, and the corner farthest from the entrance was so narrow and ended so far back that it looked as though the only way to squeeze into it was sideways, pulling in your stomach with all your might. And the inhabitant of this strange room (from the street, the building looked a little like a ship, a brick ship with a narrow prow, cleaving an intersection into two parts) was proud of it, couldn't be more content. This was the first dwelling of her very own, coming as it did after the orphanage, where she'd ended up at age five, and also after many years spent in workers' dormitories.

Sometime later, I'd made up my mind to move in with her—the garret dweller continued in his own words—when one day she stopped me short with the statement, "Doesn't it seem to you that we're courting disaster?" Having said this, she smiled, as she always did, broadly, displaying her white teeth, the tiny yellowish sparks in her eyes. The question distressed me because it also characterized perfectly some of my own vague forebodings. Though, to be sure, what's the point of talking about disaster when you're only twenty-one, and she's twenty-two (she turned out to be a year older), and neither of you have obligations, no war is going on, and you're happy with one another?

One time I returned to my garret to get back to my much-neglected textbooks and, knowing that she would be working at night, went to the window and parted the curtains. My girlfriend was at her place, and out of habit she waved to me, smiled . . . and suddenly, freezing for a moment, stared fixedly at me, the smile disappearing from her face. The face became incredibly sad. Brightly illuminated by strong lights, it looked alien and unfamiliar. I looked at her, too, for a long time without pausing. In this strange examination of one another, there was a merciless candor that neither she nor I had known before.

Then something happened that had to happen. At the beginning of summer, I left town with a student construction brigade, coming back only at the end of September. To tell the truth, I did not particularly miss my girl when I was living on the state farm and building a swine complex with fellow student friends. But, having returned to Moscow, I rushed to her with joyous impatience, to her funny building that looked like a brick ship. The house was located on one of those quiet crooked lanes of old Moscow, not far from the Crimean Bridge, and from the yard over some masonry walls located much farther down, you could catch sight of the silvery luster of the Moscow River. The building is no longer there. In its place something concrete and glass, scientific research-looking has emerged. The famous brick ship has sunk in the ocean of time.

My girlfriend, it turned out, was in the hospital, and, what's more, in one of those no one is allowed to visit, not even family and close friends. We looked at each other through a window. I stood down below on the street among visitors shouting things, cupping their hands to their mouths, she in a ward on the second floor. Pregnancy had distorted her looks a great deal. Moreover, she'd cut her hair short, that is, she'd simply hacked off the hair right below the ears and her hair, unbleached, looked pretty dark. Her large belly was clearly visible to me from below. The only thing I could really understand from the note she threw out the airing window was that she'd decided to have the child, and that her pregnancy had not been entirely trouble-free. I hadn't even known she was pregnant. Having waved in the familiar way, she disappeared.

That fall a freestyle wrestler friend from Novokuznetsk came to Moscow for the freestyle wrestling championship, and for a whole week we went to watch the matches. When the friend left to go back home to Siberia, I'd had my fill of athletic events and halfheartedly set out for the hospital. There was no reason, I thought, to burden my conscience with what in all probability other men ought to answer for. I'd been away from Moscow nearly four months. She'd said nothing about anything like this when I was leaving. We hadn't exchanged letters during that time. And even now, did she as much as hint in the note that she was expecting *our* child? "I'm expecting a child. Things are not going too well. They'll keep me under observation until the end" is all she communicated in the note. But then I recalled how she'd said to me time and again, "I'm a free woman. I'll live the way I choose." OK, I respected her views and believed that this is the way she'd always live. There were early wrinkles on her face, but they didn't make her look old. She spoke with a slight burr, but that was very becoming to her. I'd felt good with her from the very first day. Nonetheless, did this really mean that I had to act as "duty enjoins"?

I shall never forget that trip, first on the subway, then the long ride on the trackless trolley. A fall slush lay on the streets, the sky got very cloudy, and people's faces seemed to me to be too open; the imprint of some kind of knowledge, cheerless and yet needed by no one, lay on these faces. And now as I sit in my old garret, and parked down below next to the building is my car in which I've just completed a sentimental journey backward in time, I have no reason to lie to you, my dear garret dweller. Do the streets of Moscow that change beyond recognition every hundred years really need this? Does this branch of an April tree with knots and buds filled with the impatient energy of new activity need our much-touted prudence? But on that day I decided to meet and talk with my pregnant girlfriend. I went to the hospital office, with effort got permission to visit, and, after pulling on a white smock given me in the coatroom, proceeded to locate the designated ward. I was only given permission to summon the patient into the corridor, but I forgot that, and, knocking first on the door, entered the ward. I saw a very large room, filled with a multitude of beds, and on each lay a pregnant woman. Some lay on their sides, others on their backs. They looked at me closely, uncomprehendingly. But it turned out that the one I'd come to visit was not there. She'd gone for treatment, so I left the ward quickly. I went along the corridor without any sense of where I was going. An elderly, gray-haired orderly bumped into me. Plump, pink-faced, she grabbed me by the sleeve and dragged me to the exit, scolding loudly that no one was allowed in here. I followed her submissively. And just as we were going past a door fitted with glass, I caught sight of my girlfriend being led by two nurses holding her under the arms. . . . Do you remember what her face was like, how she looked? Perhaps all the prose of life with its lack of benevolent magic and its earthy and earthen side was revealed to you at that moment, and you didn't stop, you went past, a plump, white-haired old woman dragging you by the sleeve. You went out onto the street and blended with a crowd prepared to accept the most sensible decisions.

But why did you come here and converse with the young, poor garret dweller? In addition to everything else, do you really need to justify yourself to him? Why do this, you poor devil? Isn't the fact that you left the hospital then and never ever saw that woman again enough? You then abandoned the garret, and all your life after that rolled smoothly along sensible paths—of course.

I'll sit a minute longer in the cubbyhole, listening to the noise, the rumble of the untamed city, to the sparrows chirping and crows cawing. After that I'll open the window and, leaning out over the windowsill, look down

ANATOLY KIM

196

and watch the garret dweller in his shaggy hat of rabbit fur leave to do something somewhere. I won't call to him because that would be futile. I can watch him from here, I can see him, but *he* can't see me at all! I know how his life will evolve, but how is he supposed to know about this? Somewhere, I suppose, I have a son or daughter, but I can surmise this only with uncertainty. The only thing I can say with certainty is that I now have a wife who does not want to bear children and a Zhiguli car with the running boards rusted through because I failed to apply an anticorrosive coating in time.

DOUBLE STAR

My son at first did hang gliding, and then, after vocational school, he went into the army. When he came back, he got interested in how kites fly. Launched on two strings, the tips of their frames flexible, my son says that kites adjust themselves to the force of the airflow they encounter. I don't know what his next hobby will be. Perhaps he'll master the art of flying by means of muscles alone, but, when a young man of twenty or so years doesn't want to know about anything except how to fly by means of various winged machines, his mother is bound to experience at least some anxiety. But the only thing I'm experiencing is annoyance because I've only got one room and I'm simply unable to get a good night's sleep. My son, coming back after work in the design office at his factory and not having expended his youthful energies during the day, sits at the table until midnight and draws, writes, and drafts—and prevents me from sleeping. He'll set about making a "California" kite, and then I have to help by boiling up glue, cutting out the covering, and holding the ends of the thin support strips.

Sometimes I look at this strapping guy, huge by comparison to me, and am frightened by the thought: is it indeed possible that I . . . ? At some point in the past it *was* me who with agonizing labor forced him out of myself two months premature; he was kept alive for me under a glass hood. This puny being, who looked an awful lot like a small, shriveled-up monkey, was almost incapable of life. And only after I'd given him the breast and felt the milk flowing freely into him did I first sense tenderness toward my son and perceive that we would be inseparable in this world.

Once my son asked me, "After twenty-five years of honest labor, Mama, don't you deserve something better than this ratty, one-room hole unfit for normal human habitation?" To this I replied, "To be honest, my son, I don't deserve even this. Because, though I did graduate from college by taking correspondence courses, how good a specialist am I anyway? It was impossible for me to become a real specialist because I had to take care of you when you were sick, take you to day care, to school, arrange for you to go to the children's sanitorium on the Crimean coast. . . . And do you remember the room we used to have before we got this apartment? Really, you don't remember? It was a funny room with a long, long narrow corner. You loved to crawl into the corner and sleep, sticking your head into the very end. I'd pull you out by the legs. Have you really forgotten?" "And when exactly did you find time to both study and graduate?" asked my son. "I don't remember any of this."

Those were the very years I studied. You'd sleep in the evening, my son, and I'd study. A woman without a husband generally has enough time for whatever she wants to do. But if she loves someone, all her time is spent on that love. Naturally, I didn't utter words like this in his presence. As was quite often the case, I'd start a conversation with my son and continue it later—not aloud, but to myself.

He doesn't remember the old room. And, y'know, we did leave there when he was not quite three. Well, if that's so, then he doesn't remember either the rusty pail on which he hit his tender little mouth and knocked out his front teeth. It was a pail that a neighbor who was a mechanic kept junk iron and nuts in. When I begin to recall something, at times gazing off into the distance, vertigo will suddenly take hold of me. It's as if I were scudding over enormous misty spaces in some sort of flying contraption or Baba Yaga's mortar. And the point, my dear, is that there's no one in these spaces except me alone. The world of remembrances is an extinct world, where one lone soul, your own, is kept alive. But I do want to tell you, dear child, that I don't place much value on the world of my private memories. For me it's far more tempting to imagine the world you'll be living in once I'm gone.

A warm evening will set in. A sparrow will fly toward your open window, sit on the branch of a tree, and chirp. You should understand that this is me greeting you from my eternally lifeless spaces. I never wanted to be dependent on other people, especially on men. In my childhood at the orphanage I dreamed about only one thing: of sometime having a dwelling of my own, where I would admit only those I wanted to let in. And the time came when my dream was realized. I got that funny room, and into it came a man who now would be able to call himself your father. . . . When the sparrow chirps on, greeting you in my name, remember that your mother reared you by herself, without a man's help.

Remember also the times I lived in. Those times have passed, as all times do, and the mysterious dislocations of life have brought me as far as this. . . . My son, you might find it interesting to know that in the distant past luck was not always on my side, that I landed in a horrible orphanage, a real den of thieves . . . many of its workers were later brought to trial. They beat the children unmercifully, the director used us as domestics, like servants, and I, imagine, at one time slept with two little boys on bare mattresses on the floor, and one of the boys was all infested with impetigo. It was he who later grew up to become an artist. The other one died after the orphanage. He was supposed to have become an airline pilot. He and I sent money from our earnings to Akhmedich, our artist, the first of us to become a student. And after I gave birth to you, he came to take me home from the lying-in hospital, and for many years he helped us so that you and I were never wanting for anything.

It's a long time since I've heard how Akhmedich is getting along. Somehow he has no luck with women. Been married four or five times, each time unsuccessfully. It would never occur either to him or to me even to think about the possibility of conjugal ties. Most likely in those childhood days filled with foolhardy resistance and struggle, a deep brother-sister relationship developed between us. Now Akhmedich and I very rarely, and then as a rule by accident, run into each another. At first there're always tears, and these are not some kind of sentimental tears. We're both simply recalling the third member of our group, Misha Kiselev, and lamenting the fact that after all we went through he died suddenly from common pneumonia. Akhmedich was always skinny—and nearly bald since he was in his early twenties—but wiry and with broad bones, whereas Misha Kiselev was the biggest boy in the orphanage. Now when I'm on business trips and in planes and see imposing, manly pilots ("Our captain today is Pilot First Class . . . ," the stewardess will announce in a deferential tone), I think about how Misha might have been one of them.

I feel very guilty about you. I gave birth to you, but did not let you—did not want to let you—have a father. I feel particularly guilty when I see on the street somewhere the proverbial happy duo of unpretentious father, nothing special to look at, with a small beard and wearing a beret, a knapsack on his back, in his hand fishing rods taken apart and tied up in a single bundle. Behind this organized father minces along a pale child of the city, in glasses, a silly happy smile pasted on his face. You can see right away that great adventures await both mighty father and tiny fisherman, and that there will also perhaps be a night spent by the fire on a riverbank. I probably didn't have the right to deprive my son of such joys, and this is why the sight of the man with the small beard in the beret with fishing rods in his hand won't leave me. But how could I have provided you with such an enthusiastic daddy, one who liked the sport of fishing, when men like this are rare among us, appearing only once in a blue moon? My son, you had a father, but he perished in an automobile accident shortly after you were born. Carrying you was very hard, and in the seventh month I was put into a special hospital where they send women whose pregnancies are not going well. Your father would come to visit me. . . .

I didn't remarry. At the orphanage I learned how to endure, and that's helped me hold on during difficult times, but no matter how hard things were, I never thought of making my situation easier by means of an advantageous marriage. I knew what I had to do: be at work every day possible. That way I'd get full pay; I wasn't going to go crazy like other women. My son, I remained faithful to *you*.

It's hard to imagine the time when I'll be gone and you'll still be alive, but I send my blessings for this time. Please, God, let it be a peaceful time, like that which fell to my lot after the orphanage. I came into this world in the postwar era, when people were just barely beginning to forget what lengths they would go to if threatened by death from violence or starvation. My son, I remained alone not because I was ugly, spineless, tiresome, or lacking in any other way, no. I can say to you without embarrassment: believe me, I knew something! All my life it was as if I'd preserved some higher knowledge sealed deep inside me, and I would have liked to convey it to someone. But, as it turns out, even for this knowledge to be revealed to me, there had to be an encounter with a special person. And that encounter has not taken place.

Now why is it that you never go anywhere, my son?

Why do these kites and hang gliders matter so much to you? Will inserting strips of spring steel into wing tips really make you much happier? I've lived by myself until now, and I've worked how many years for one establishment, first simply as a worker, and later, after finishing college by correspondence, as an engineer. I've received a separate apartment, a plot in the country. *Cogito ergo sum,* etc. . . . But to tell the truth, my son, I didn't need to live this way. I'd like to tell you, and maybe one day I'll have the nerve to tell you, that living this way wasn't worth it. My whole life was spent on trifles of one sort or another, although I really tried not to squander my talents and chase after chimeras. Probably I wasn't good at being happy because I didn't want happiness. Yes, that's right, I didn't want it. After the childhood that befell me, I have to be honest and admit that I can't really look at happy people without entertaining suspicions. It's impossible for me to avoid thinking that any happiness has to be paid for by someone else's unhappiness. I learned to think in this logical way later, when there was time to reflect on such matters. But at the time I was young, and I decided to keep my child and say nothing to the poor student (knowing in advance what he'd go through, though it's possible he'd have said nothing out loud—it seemed like he really loved me). In those years, I didn't even think about great happiness and merely avoided everyone, everyone in whose eyes I could detect even fleeting anxiety or who concealed the hostility people leading a trouble-free existence feel when they find themselves among those whose lives are not trouble-free. I got my fill of people like this in the hungry, postwar period, when we orphans ran away as we often did from our institutional home and begged at nearby summer cottages and villages.

They were helping me walk back to the ward after a blood transfusion, something I always withstood poorly, when beyond the glass door that separated the treatment rooms from the corridor I saw the face of a young man who in the eyes of God and man was husband to me and father to my future child. It was his face I didn't like. At first he didn't see me—I saw him. But then I turned away, pretending I hadn't noticed him. He, of course, did catch sight of me. However, he didn't stop and didn't call to me. And I think about how people who are in fact strangers to each other and who know virtually nothing at all about each other, who have nothing in common, and who are grossly incompatible, sometimes call themselves husband and wife, a family, and often live together till death, God!

Once I said to my son: "Do you think that happiness is going to simply fall into your hands all by itself like some rosy ripe apple? Why do you spend all your time here with your mother? You have to seek . . . really . . . you have to search carefully for the right person for yourself. But all you do is hang around home, gluing California kites together." You're going to spend so much time here that one day you'll start thinking: man was created to be all by himself and all by himself he must stay. This will become the norm, and all possible unions on earth between men and women will seem to you to be nothing more than a terrible and agonizing misunderstanding. And then, my son, know that all is lost. For you'll be embarking on an existence without happiness, perhaps a long and prosperous existence, in which it'll seem right to keep your distance from those who call their mutual state of torment family life. And even from those filled with the confusion of life's daily tribulations you'll be eternally separated by a zone of alienation, a forbidden area through which your solitude will never dare pass. I wanted to be a free woman, one who knew not that cruel deceit that often lies at the base of decent family well-being (too early did I become familiar with how one person can be an unbearable tormentor of another). So I became a free woman, independent and alone, just as I had imagined. But I advise you to flee as far as possible from this woman so full of good intentions and find yourself a pretty girlfriend, understanding and unaffected, and with her experience all that I've avoided so prudently. I'm one of those people who in our difficult times chose out of fear that which is most humble and unassuming: a simple existence, simply living and breathing, looking at the world and being present in it. Only a person who has been through the school of hard knocks consents very readily to an existence without happiness, to a long life lacking the sublime. My son, get away from me before it's too late.

When I decided to have you, I was motivated by the usual considerations of this world: a woman should give birth; I didn't want to be married, yet I wanted a child. Of course, I assumed that it would not be easy, but at the same time I also knew something else—that after a while everything would sort itself out, and my child would become the purpose and justification for my entire existence. However, I didn't contemplate that you would shoot up to be twice the size of your mother, that it would be nothing for you to turn over all the soil of our plot in the country by yourself, and that you'd suddenly rise into the air on a winged contraption.

Of course I was flattered. I cried all night after what my son said to me one day in response to my words. "Mother, for the time being I don't need your young ladies," he said. "So why do you badger me about them? Now just where am I supposed to bring one of these young ladies? To our one-room hole, huh? But Mother, that's not the point. Keep your cool. Just the two of us alone together isn't so bad, is it? I wouldn't mind, of course, if someone like you were to come along, but where can you find such a girl? You and I, we're like a double star. Without a telescope you can't tell that we're separate bodies. It's our business to shine unobtrusively, but you keep sending me to socials at the Technicians Hall. What the hell do I need this Technicians Hall for? All they do there is make you dance the rumba and calypso."

His words, of course, went straight to my heart, but what good was this star if there'd been nothing in me to shine for a long time? Good lord, just think of the year my boy went to school. What sort of star was I then? All I could think of was how I should dash home as early as possible, because after school my son would be roaming aimlessly about the courtyard hungry. I didn't permit him to use the gas range. I preferred giving him money for dinner so he could go eat at a dumpling shop. However, I had strong suspicions that the boy spent the money on ice cream. If a single mother has anything to shine, it's her

crazy eyes from her crazy worry that her child is loung-
ing about somewhere without any supervision.

Yes, I lived the way I wanted and in my own way was
probably happy. However, any happiness in this world is
sullied by the touch of the unhappy. Let's say I'm weeding
the strawberries on a hot day. I stand after bending over
the bed of plants wearing a bathing suit, my head covered
with a straw hat. It's so nice! A cool breeze caresses my
shoulders. My son has done a good job of sharpening the
hoe. Good lord, what more could you ask for. . . . Then
suddenly I recall the old Buryat woman whom I saw in
the morning as I was approaching the metro station at a
brisk pace, knapsack on my back. As soon as it gets
warm, this neglected, unkempt Buryat woman appears by
the metro and sits the whole day long on a crude, gray,
wooden box where the cleanup people keep their
brooms, dustpans, and shovels. I heard she has a daughter in Moscow, someone with an education. The crowd
flows about, the old woman mumbles something in her
own language and, having pulled her scarf down to her
very nose, rocks from side to side. Sometimes, leaning her
back against the tree right next to the box, she sleeps,
dropping her gray head on her breast and snoring loudly.
I'm not trying to say that my recollection of this neglected Buryat woman deprives me of my feeling of happiness
brought on by the fine day and peaceful work, but, if an
old woman like this exists anywhere in the whole wide
world, then it can't help but affect my happy feelings
about life. Over my lifetime, starting with the orphanage,
I've accumulated quite a few recollections of this sort.

Could I really have married *him?* He was a tall, good-looking fellow, with no-nonsense glasses and very short hair. His nose was the only thing I didn't particularly like. It was thin and for some reason very hard, actually horn-like, like a bird's beak. When he got mad, gristly blue patches would appear on the tip of his nose and over his pale nostrils. At times like that I was afraid of him. What he made of himself in life, I don't know, but that isn't important. Anyhow, I know what he might have become. He was one of those men who, wanting to separate from their wives, do so with agonizing doubts, subsequently sink into even greater doubts, and end up returning. That's of course in cases where the old wives will take them back. If I'd married him then, I'd probably have lived in a four-room apartment and my plot in the country would have been a little closer to Moscow than the one I have now. I'd be the wife of a man who lacked self-confidence, who probably would not be a bad specialist at whatever he did, but who when faced with poverty, disaster, or death would be totally unable to react in the way you'd like him to. For some reason, I think too much about him and, as always, it doesn't make sense to me. However, there've also been many other men I've met in my life who've not inspired enough confidence in me to marry them. Quite frankly, only one man has seemed to me to be entirely worthy of a woman's respect, and that's my flyer-man, my double star, my wonderful son, for me the most mysterious man of all.

L U D M I L A   U L I T S K A Y A

MARCH SECOND
OF *THAT* YEAR

Winter was horrible. The cold was especially damp and bitter. It was like an especially dirty quilt weighing down the shoulders of a low-hanging sky. Great-grandfather, bedridden since fall, was dying slowly on the narrow couch upholstered in carpet material. He looked around affectionately with sunken yellowish gray eyes and did not remove the phylacteries from his left arm. With his right hand, he pressed against his stomach a flat, electric hot water bottle encased in worn gray serge. The epitome of technological progress at the beginning of the century, it had been brought from Vienna by his son, Alexander, before the First World War, when he returned home as a young professor of medicine after studying abroad for eight years.

As a matter of fact, applying heat to the old man's stomach had been strictly forbidden, but beneath this weak, inanimate warmth the pain subsided, and the oncologist son finally acceded to the old man's request and let him use the hot water bottle. The son was well aware of both the tumor's size and the area that was metastasizing—conditions that ruled out an operation. He admired the quiet fortitude of a father who in his entire ninety-year existence had not complained about anything nor ever been resentful.

Great-granddaughter Lily, with her shining brown eyes and matte black hair, was the apple of his eye. She'd come home from school in her brown uniform stained with chalk dust and violet ink. Affectionate, rosy-natured, she'd climb onto the couch next to the side of him that hurt, pull the afghan up over herself, moving around her elbows and chubby knees, and whisper into great-grand-father's hairy, emaciated ear, "So tell me a story."

And old Aaron would tell a story, about Daniel or about Gideon, or about bogatyrs, beautiful women, sages, and tsars with hard to pronounce names. All were their kin who had died long ago, but the little girl was under the impression that Great-grandfather Aaron, because he was so old, had known and remembered some of them.

For Lily, too, this winter was horrible. She, too, felt the unusual heaviness of the sky, the low spirits at home, and the hostility of the air on the streets. She was in her twelfth year. Her armpits hurt and her nipples itched in a disgusting way. At times, a wave of loathing rolled over her from those small swellings, the coarse dark little hairs, the tiniest pimples on her forehead—and her whole being blindly objected to all these unpleasant, unclean changes in her body. Every single thing was simply filled with repugnance—like the greasy, carroty-orange film on mushroom soup, the boring Gedike she tormented daily on the cold piano, the scratchy woolen pants she pulled on in the morning, the deadly lavender covers of her school notebooks. And only by the side of her great-grandfather, who smelled of camphor and old paper, was she free of this burdensome obsession.

Grandmother Bella Zinovievna, professor and specialist in skin diseases, and Alexander Aaronovich were a indefatigable couple; together they pulled a sizeable load. Alexander Aaronovich, "Surik" to those at home, was a tall, bony, and big-eared man. Author of uncomplicated jokes and highly complex surgical operations, he loved to say that he'd committed his entire life to two women: Bella and Lady Medicine. The shortish, plump Bella, with her penciled eyebrows, lips smeared with red lipstick, and bright gray hair, wasn't afraid of her competition.

A strange kind of agitation affected them both when, coming home from work, they found the old man and young girl so engrossed in each other. They'd exchange glances, and Bella would brush a tear away from the corner of her mascaraed eye. Surik would tap his fingers on the table in a meaningful and admonishing way. Bella would raise an open palm, as if using sign language for deaf-mutes. They had a great many such motions, signs, secret wordless ways of communication, so that there was little need for them to speak; they caught everything by mutual waves of affection.

"Our old father is departing," is what these still-young oldsters understood, "and at death's door is transferring his dubious wealth to the younger generation, our little girl who's on the verge of puberty." And although to the learned professors the Old Testament tales about those ancient people seemed to be the naive and worn-out clothing of human thought, although their way of thinking had been shaped by and disciplined in the Viennese and Zurich school of European positivism, although they were trained to take part in clever scholarly polemics, and although they worshiped but one cardboard god—the slippery fact—and steadfastly adhered to an atheism both honest and sorrowful, nonetheless both felt that here on the worn couch, next to a death indulgently unhurried, flourished an extraordinary oasis. Here were none of those physicians who poisoned people, nor was there present that mystical fear of criminal intent that now gripped millions. Here alone the spirit of this real poison, the fear, vileness, and evildoing, was in retreat. And this is why the learned professors, depressed and prepared every day for arrest, exile, or anything, were slow to leave the dining room, their common room where the old man ailed, to busy themselves with their normal research. Instead, they sat down in armchairs next to that then rarest of rarities, a television—not turned on, by the way—and listened attentively to the old man's songlike cooing. He was speaking about Mordecai and Haman. They exchanged smiles, felt sad, and kept silent about that madness they plunged into every day beyond the threshold of their home.

They'd lived through the Great War, losing brothers, nephews, and numerous relatives, but they had preserved each other, their small family, total mutual trust, friendship, and tenderness, and they'd achieved success that was real yet not blatant. You'd imagine they could've lived another full decade in the way they'd always wanted if their health, strength, and worldly wisdom remained in happy equilibrium—working an entire, overscheduled week with relish; leaving on Saturday to spend Sunday at the new, recently completed summer cottage; playing Schubert four-hands on a rather bad cottage instrument; bathing after dinner in a dark, water-lilied brook; drinking tea from the samovar on the wooden veranda in the slanting rays of the setting sun; in the evening, reading Dickens or Mérimée. They'd fall asleep at the same time, hugging one another as they had for forty odd years, and you couldn't tell whether the convex and concave shapes of their bodies in fixed positions guaranteed their steady comfort or, if over the years they'd spent in nightly embrace, the bodies themselves had changed shape to accommodate each other, to form this unity.

And you'd have thought their cup of life-darkening sorrows was full, more than enough for their gray heads, because of the long-standing and painful conflict with their son who'd voluntarily chosen a field to which the devil couldn't attract a normal person for love or money. The son held an important but undefined post, and lived in northeast Russia beyond the Arctic Circle together with his bearlike wife, Shura, and young son, Alexander. What a mockery of fate that two people who couldn't have less in common in one family had the same first name.

In 1943, their son had brought his older child, Lily, to Vyatka, to the military hospital where his parents labored at the operating table day after day twelve hours at a stretch. The baby was then five months old. She weighed three kilograms and looked like a dried-up doll. From that day on until the very end of the war, the two worked different shifts; usually Alexander Aaronovich chose nights. Lily, made better and nourished by Bella Zinovievna, remained with her grandmother and grandfather for good, as if born anew for the glorious destiny of being the granddaughter of professors. But, aware of the touchiness of her real mother, Shura, who came from time to time, Lily called her foster parents "Bella" and "Surik," and her great-grandfather, "Grandfather."

Now Bella and Surik sat in soft old armchairs slipcovered in unbleached linen, turned part way toward the couch. They pretended they weren't listening to what the old man and the young girl were whispering about.

"Grandpa," Lily said horrified, "you mean that they hanged all of those enemies from a tree?"

"What I don't say to you is: 'This is bad, this is good.' I'm telling you what happened," her great-grandfather replied, with regret in his voice.

"Others will come and wreak vengeance. They'll kill Mordecai . . . ," said the little girl sadly.

"Well, naturally." For some unknown reason greatgrandfather was exuberant. "Naturally, that's just what happened later on. Other people came, killed these people, and then the same thing over again. In general, you should understand that Israel lives on not by victory, Israel lives on . . . ," he put his left arm with the phylacteries to his forehead and raised his fingers upward, "do you understand?"

"By the will of God?"

"Didn't I always say that you're a clever girl," smiled grandfather Aaron with a completely toothless, childlike mouth.

"Do you hear what he's stuffing the child's head with?" Bella sadly asked her husband when they were in their own room with, as Surik joked, their double bed of a desk.

"Bella dear, my father's only a simple cobbler. But it's not up to me to teach him. Y'know, sometimes I think that it would have been better if I'd become a cobbler," said Surik gloomily.

"What are you talking about? You're not allowed to go backward!" the reasonable Bella replied, irritated.

"Then you shouldn't go 'n' get upset on account of little Lily," he said grinning.

"OK." Bella gave up. She was practical and not given to thought this elevated. "That's not what I'm really afraid of. I'm afraid that she'll blurt something out at school."

"My dear! But that isn't important anymore," said Surik, shrugging his shoulders.

•   •   •

Bella Zinovievna worried unnecessarily. Lily could not possibly have blurted anything out. Ever since fall, no one in her class had talked to her. No one that is except Ninka Kniazev, who was forever being transferred to a school for the handicapped, except they could never get the paperwork completed. Big, exceptionally beautiful, contrary to northern types, Ninka had matured early. She was the one girl in the class who because of her simple-mindedness not only greeted Lily, but was even glad to be her partner when this chirping flock of schoolchildren was taken on some required trip to a museum awarded the Order of the Red Banner.

The time had its ingrained habits: Tartars were friends with Tartars, "C" pupils with "C" pupils, doctors' children with doctors' children . . . the children of Jewish doctors in particular. Such a petty, such a ridiculous caste system as this would have been unknown even in ancient India. Lily was left without a girlfriend. Tanya Kogan, a neighbor and classmate, had been sent off to relatives in Riga even before New Year's, so the last two months had been totally unbearable for Lily.

Any outburst of laughter, any boisterous behavior, any whispering—to Lily, it all seemed directed against her. The suspicious buzzing she heard around her was invariably the beetlelike buzzing, the blackish-brown "jooz," which crept out of the word "Jew-girl." And most tormenting of all was that this dark, sticky, and pitchlike atmosphere was connected with their last name, with Grandfather Aaron, with his fragrant, leather-bound books, with the honey and cinnamon smell of the East and the undulating golden light that always surrounded him, filling the entire left corner of the room where he lay.

Moreover, both of these feelings, the golden luminescence at home and the brown buzzing outside, were forever linked in an inscrutable way. . . .

Hoarse and long-awaited, the liberator bell barely had a chance to ring when Lily whisked her exemplary notebooks into her satchel and rushed on heavy legs to the coatroom, so that, without fastening the buttons and that spiteful little hook at the very top of her coat, she could spring ever so quickly out into the fresh air and dart rapidly through the lumps of snow-gray mush, through puddles with broken ice, her stockings and coat hem getting splashed from galoshes barely kept on, through yet one more courtyard, and then into her own entryway with its soothing smell of damp lime, up the stairway to the second floor minus a landing with the smooth bend leading to the high black door where the warm copper plate with the name Zhizhmorsky—their horrid, impossible, shameful name—was to be found.

Lately, yet another trial had been added. At the schoolyard exit, swinging himself on the very high and rusty gate, a frightening person, Vitka Bodrov, or "Bodrik" as everybody called him, lay in wait for her. He had tin-colored dark blue eyes and a common face.

The game was not complicated. There was only one exit from the schoolyard, through this very gate. When Lily would approach it, trying to burrow her way more tightly into the crowd, wily classmates would either step back slightly or run along ahead, and when she got to the dangerous spot, Bodrik would push with his foot and, letting her go forward just a bit, aim the gate with its revolting squeak at her back. The blow was not painful, but insulting. Every day added something new to the game. Once Lily turned around in order to receive the blow not with her back but her face. She grabbed the iron bars of the gate and hung on them for a while.

Another time, she stopped some distance away from the gate and waited a long while, pretending she didn't intend to go home. But Bodrik had more than enough patience and spare time and, having detained her this way for about half an hour, watched with pleasure as she tried to push herself between the bars of the fence. This attempt failed. The skinniest of girls could hardly have squeezed through the narrow space, much less someone wearing a thick coat to make the situation worse.

There was the lucky day she managed to gallop in front of an old teacher named Antonina Vladimirovna, whose east Siberian face showed great astonishment at this display of bad manners.

The entertainment became more appealing day after day. Everyone who did not mind taking the time gathered to watch. The number of spectators grew from day to day. Just yesterday they'd been rewarded by a thrilling spectacle. Lily had made a desperate and nearly successful attempt to climb over the school fence, which was topped by flat iron spikes. First she shoved her satchel through the bars, and then she put her foot in a place she had picked out in advance, a place where a few of the bars were bent. She climbed up to the very top, threw one leg over, then the second, only to realize that she had made a mistake in not starting the other way round. Frightened to death, she turned the other way, and slowly slid down pressing her face against the rusty iron.

The skirt of her coat caught on a spike and stretched. At first she did not understand what held her back, then she tugged. The honest twill from the coat of an old professor, turned and altered and now living out its life on a chubby youthful body, strained and offered resistance, each of its high-quality twisted threads fully taut. The enthusiastic audience began to buzz. Like a big heavy bird, Lily tugged, and the coat released her with a raspy snap. When she dropped to the ground, Bodrik stood next to her, holding in his hands the soiled satchel and smiling warmly.

"Well done, Lil. You did it. Gonna climb up again?"

With the feint of a hunter, he tossed her satchel as if effortlessly but with a hand as accurate as that of an Australian aborigine. Up it soared, rocking from side to side, turned in the air, and plopped down on the other side of the fence. Everyone began to laugh.

Lily picked her little woolen hat with its two stupid tails off the ground and, without a backward glance, straining with all her might not to run, walked home. They didn't come after her. Half an hour later the loyal Ninka brought her the satchel, which had been wiped dry with a handkerchief, and shoved it into the door.

The next morning, Lily pretended to be sick, complaining about her throat. Bella Zinovievna looked in her mouth in a cursory way, stuck the thermometer under her armpit, caught the disappearing column of mercury with a glimpse of her eye and, displeased, pronounced her verdict: "Get up, young lady. You have to work. Everyone has to work."

Work was Bella Zinovievna's religion. The blasphemy of laziness she did not tolerate. Despondent, Lily dragged herself to school and sat through three periods, agonizing about the unavoidable passage through the gates of Hell. Then, during the fourth period something happened.

It was only the second of March, and the steering wheel of the unsinkable ship had yet to leave the hands of the Great Helmsman, Stalin. Had Alexander Aaronovich and Bella Zinovievna known about this incredible act from the secretive Lily, they would have valued it highly.

And so, during the fourth period, near the end,

Antonina Vladimirovna, her eyes, the most inspired part of her face, aglow, her steel teeth in shiny metallic dialogue with the silver pin in the shape of a twisted pretzel-like turd at her collar, took the polished, one-and-a-half-meter pointer in her hands and proceeded to the dusty, colorful chart at the back of the classroom. Holding the pointer like a rapier, she struck with its tip the immutable word "International."

"Look over here, children." That's just how she would address them, "children," not the old-fashioned secondary-school word "girls," nor the impersonal "students." On the chart were depicted representatives of all the peoples of our great multinational motherland. "See, here are Russians and Ukrainians and Georgians and . . ." Lily was sitting turned half around in a state of quiet terror. Was she really about to pronounce that which would cause the entire class to turn toward her? ". . . and Tartars," continued the teacher. Everyone turned toward Raya Akhmetov, whose face flushed dark red. And Antonina Vladimirovna raced along the dangerous path: ". . . and Armenians and Azerbijanies . . . " That's just what she said, "Azerbijanies." She's going to pass by it, she is . . . . No! ". . . and Jews!"

Lily was petrified. The whole class turned around in her direction.

Sacred simplicity personified, an intellectual commoner through and through, her grandfather a sacristan, her mother a washerwoman, Antonina Vladimirovna was a chaste virgin—with a medical certification of *virgina intacta*—who during the war had adopted an orphan, the squinty-eyed and malicious Zoika. Admiring Chernyshevky and adoring Klara Zetkin, Rosa Luxemburg, and Nadezhda Krupskaya, she had a prophetic, feminist vein in her. Believing in "primary matter," as her grandfather sacristan had believed in the Precious Mother of God, and honest as the day is long, she was firm in her knowledge that enemies will be enemies, but Jews are only Jews.

However, at the time Lily did not understand the magnitude of this action. To her painted desk she pressed the gap of bare skin left by her stockings, which were too short, and the tight rubber band of her hateful light blue drawers with their ticklish Chinese fuzzy-napped insides.

"All nationalities are equal in our country," said Antonina Vladimirovna, continuing her sacred task as teacher. "There are no bad nationalities. Each nationality has its own heroes as well as its own criminals, and even enemies of the people. . . ."

She said something more, something tedious, superfluous, but Lily did not hear her. Lily felt some tiny vein throbbing next to her nose and with her finger she touched this spot, wondering if its twitching would be noticed by Svetka Bagaturiya, who sat across the aisle from her.

•   •   •

At the school gate a stroke of good luck awaited Lily: no Bodrik. With a sense of complete and everlasting freedom and without a single thought about his possible reappearance even the day after tomorrow, she rushed home skipping. The outside door, usually held firmly closed by a tight spring, was open just slightly, but Lily paid no attention to this. She flung it open and, stepping from the light into the darkness, could distinguish only the dark silhouette of a person standing by the inside door. It was Bodrik. He had been holding the door slightly open with his foot so that he could see in advance anyone coming in. Separating them now were two meters of complete darkness, but somehow she saw that it was he who was standing there, his back pressed against the inside door, his arms spread out as on a cross, his head with its thick light brown hair bent to one side.

He was an actor, this Bodrik, and now he was playing a role both awesome and important. He thought he was impersonating Christ, but in fact he was a petty, insolent, miserable thief. And the girl stood opposite him, with her mournful Semitic face: her thin, high-bridged nose, the outside corners of her eyes turned downward, a mouth gently protruding. The very same face that Joseph's Mary had. . . .

"What did your Jews crucify our Christ for?" he asked spitefully. He asked this as if the Jews had crucified this Christ solely to give him, Bodrik, the full and sacred right to smack Lily on her backside with the rusty iron gate.

Lily froze in anticipation. She seemed to forget that she could rush outside and immediately run away. After all, the outside door was in back of her. She stood there in a stupor, goodness knows why.

Bodrik stepped up to her, grabbed hold of her firmly, slid his hands down and lifted up her unbuttoned coat, his hand coming right up against that bare space between her stockings and the rubber band of the drawers that she wore pulled up to her very crotch.

She wriggled free, rushed over into the corner, jabbed Bodrik in some unresisting spot with her satchel. He groaned, and she rushed outside, her fingers immediately catching the door handle despite the total darkness. A dense pink flame blazed in her head, all the air around caught fire, and everything was inundated with such a mighty, red-hot rage that she began to tremble. She could barely contain the enormity of this feeling which had neither name nor limit.

The door slowly opened. Bodrik emerged, one shoulder first, moving slightly sideways. Lily threw herself on him, grabbing him by the shoulders, and with a howl threw him against the door with all her might. The attack took him completely by surprise. The complex feelings for her he had long harbored—a mixture of craving, anger, and unrecognized envy at her well-fed and clean life—could not compare in terms of strength and inner justification to that fiery outburst of fury which now raged in her soul.

He tried to tear her away, to shake her off, but that proved impossible. He couldn't even swing his arm the way he needed to in order to hit her. He succeeded only in moving around the corner by the entrance door into a hidden recess in the wall where they could not be seen by anyone crossing the yard. But this did not make things better. She shook him by the shoulders. His head knocked against the rough, gray masonry. His teeth were chattering, and the only thing that he was able to do was to free one arm and to strike her moist red face twice, and even then not in a "manly" way with his fist but with all five fingers spread out—leaving four crude and dirty scratches on her face. But she didn't feel this. She kept throwing him against the wall until suddenly her fury, like an inflated red balloon, detached itself from her and flew away. She let go of him and, turning her unprotected back to him with nary a thought about a rear attack, proceeded to her own entrance door unimpeded.

•　　•　　•

How she'd liked him last summer. She'd stood behind the lace curtains of her grandmother's room for hours and observed him swinging a long pole with a fluttering rag on the end. His doves, rising lazily, at first hovered over the dovecote as a disorderly, slovenly bunch, and then, coming together, made smooth wide circles, ever wider and wider, and flew into the cleanly washed warm sky. Walking past their dwelling, a low, two-windowed structure with an attached dovecote, shed, and hen-coop, she would slacken her pace, watching the fascinating interior of the private life of strangers: their steel barrels, the bench at which Bodrov senior would work when on temporary release from his usual prison habitat, a rusty, water pipe removed from somewhere lying on the ground. . . .

At the end of the summer Bella Zinovievna, steadfastly fulfilling some kind of anachronistic obligation of rich people to poor known only to her, had sent Lily to the home of the woman janitor, carrying a fiercely ironed, neatly folded stack of little Lily's things, which she had grown out of so swiftly that year. With squeals and much noise, the Bodrov girls, Ninka and Nyushka, divided up Lily's clothing. Tonka, the janitor, said "Thank you" and thrust a small green cucumber into Lily's hand, while

Bodrik, who had caught sight of Lily from a distance as she approached, slipped away to his doves, rabbits, and chickens. The whole time Lily was in their enclosure, which was fenced off from the rest of the yard, Bodrik did not show himself. Lily kept glancing in that direction to see if he wasn't going to appear.

Only now, at her front door, did she understand that this was really the most awful thing of all.

•   •   •

Old Nastya, who had lived with them some twenty years, wasn't home. Great-grandfather, to whom Lily rushed, was sleeping unconcernedly, snoring from time to time. Lily found refuge in her grandmother's room, on the "sorrowful little sofa," as Bella Zinovievna called the loveseat, the only unpaired item in this paired kingdom, where everything was doubled as if the room were partitioned lengthwise by an invisible mirror. There were two majestic bedsteads with bronze fittings, two matching bedside tables, and two identical frames with pictures in them that were scarcely different. Lily usually slept on this "sorrowful little sofa" when she was sick, when her grandmother took her into her room. And it was here that Lily came to cry when something distressing happened in her childhood life.

Now she was feverish, the bottom part of her belly ached, and she curled up on the little sofa, pulling up over her head the heavy checkered robe bound with a violet woven cord that had come unstitched in places. She wanted to sleep, and fell asleep instantly. The thought "How I want to sleep" remained in her head, not leaving her even while she slept.

Her sleep, though long, had nonetheless all congealed into a single strain of nagging pain and infinite loathing. A loathing for the rough fabric of the sofa cushion, for the soapy, indecent underwear smell of Red Moscow, her grandmother's favorite perfume. And all this was eclipsed by an immense desire to flee it all for some round, warm, long-familiar cranny, and there fall into a deeper sleep, a sleep that knew no smells, no pain, no worrisome shame coming from nobody knows where. She wanted to flee to where there was nothing, absolutely nothing. She didn't hear the muffled bustling on the other side of the wall next to her grandfather, Nastya's sobs, or the quiet tinkling of the syringe.

It was late, eight o'clock in the evening, when her grandmother woke her. It turned out that she'd really managed to go quite far away because, waking up, at first she couldn't understand where she was. From such a long, long way off she returned to her grandmother's room, to that symmetrically paired and proportioned world, and was astonished by the bright face bent over her. It was as if the face had been turned upside down and wasn't recognizable, as if the wide expanses of sleep she'd been in were by nature so convincing in their singularity that they precluded even the possibility of things being paired or symmetrical in any way.

Bella Zinovievna, for her part, was examining in astonishment the four fresh scratches that went from Lily's forehead across her cheeks and right down to her chin.

"Good Lord, Lily. What happened to your face?" she asked.

For a minute the girl pondered. How completely she'd forgotten what had happened during the day. Then it came to the surface, all at once, all that had happened the previous week and last summer, but it came to the surface in a completely unrecognizable form, one which made it insignificant. It was all mere nonsense, an insignificant trifle, an event half-forgotten from a long, long time ago.

"Nothing much. Fought with Bodrik," Lily answered in a lighthearted way, smiling with a sleepy face.

"How come you fought?" Bella Zinovievna questioned again.

"Just some stupid things, why we'd crucified Christ." Lily smiled.

"What?" exclaimed Bella Zinovievna, knitting her black eyebrows. And, not waiting for an answer, she ordered Lily to get dressed immediately.

A reflection of that anger which had seized Lily near the outside door now swept over her grandmother.

"How mean. What black ingratitude," Bella Zinovievna seethed. She dragged a resisting Lily by the hand to the Bodrovs' dwelling. After all, it wasn't a matter of the neat thirty rubles in notes, or the little stacks of Lily's old yet still quite decent things, which Bella Zinovievna punctually presented at holidays to this degraded, unhappy drunk of a woman. Rather, it was a matter of how according to her symmetrical understanding of fairness, Tonka's son had no right to raise his hand against her clean, cheerful girl, against her swarthy pink little face, how he had no right to insult her with his dirty fingers, with these horrid scratches. By the way, she should have washed them thoroughly with peroxide. . . .

Bella Zinovievna knocked and, without waiting for a response, flung open the crooked door. In the room with its big stove and damp underwear hanging on low-stretched clotheslines at first you couldn't make out even who and what was where. The smell was worse than that from Red Moscow, coming as it did from the most frightening poverty imaginable—urine, rot, mold, and slimy goo.

"Tonya!" called Bella Zinovievna in a commanding voice, and behind the stove something began to rustle.

Lily looked around. The floor surprised her most of all. It was dirt, covered here and there with uneven boards. In the corner, on a wide iron bed with rusty rods, just like those in the school fence, lay Bodrik on a motley-colored quilt. At his feet sat Ninka and Nyushka. They were winding wide crumpled ribbons around the bedstead, carefully moistening them with spit each time around. On the floor next to the bed was a crooked basin, no longer round.

From behind the stove, emerged a slightly unsteady, smallish Tonka, putting her skirt in order as she moved. "Here I am, Belzinovna!" She was smiling, and each cheek of her wide, flat face was indented with a dimple, round and large, like a belly button.

"Now you look right here at what your Victor did to my little girl!" said Bella Zinovievna sternly, while Tonya goggled with her whitish eyes and couldn't for the life of her understand what exactly he'd done. In the dim light, the scratches so insulting to Bella Zinovievna weren't really visible. Lily backed up to the threshold. She was ashamed. Vitka shook his head, leaned over the bed, and quietly puked into the basin.

"Oh, what a curse you are!" shouted Tonka, turning toward her son. "Now get up. What're ya lazing 'round in bed for?"

They were both silent as they passed through the yard. Lily again trailed behind, and again she felt as miserable as she had earlier that day when she'd fallen sound asleep. At home she went to their small bathroom, locked herself in with the hook, and sat on the toilet, clasping her aching stomach with her hands. Never had she felt so badly. She looked at her lowered drawers and saw on their sky-blue color a bloody spot like a tulip.

"I'm dying," thought the girl. "It's so horrid, and I'm so ashamed."

At that moment she'd forgotten everything her grandmother had warned her about. With loathing she pulled the stained drawers off, shoved them under the overturned pail used for washing the floors, and, lowering her scratch-covered face into her cold hands, with a sinking heart began to wait for her death.

• • •

And death, urged on by its expectation, was actually entering the house. On the couch upholstered in carpet material, old cobbler Aaron's breathing was uneven. He lay unconscious. His eyelids, which had long lost their eyelashes, were not tightly closed, but his eyes could not be seen—there was merely a cloudy whitish film. His withered arms lay on top of the blanket and the left one was all wound around with worn-out leather bands which, contrary to custom, he had not removed for a month. His children, professors, burdened with a great deal of medical knowledge so bulky and useless, stood at the head of his bed.

In the janitor's dwelling on the iron bed lay Bodrik. He had a mild concussion of the brain.

On a narrow couch, in his home near Moscow, half-covered by an old army blanket, lay a dead man.

But it was still only the second of March, and several enormous days would pass before Lily's father, the son of respectable parents, would come out onto a raised wooden platform and, bloated, with a heart black from grief, in innocent, light-blue shoulder boards, announce the Man's death to the gray rectangle of many thousands—that part of the great Soviet people who, because of a printing flaw, couldn't be made out at the far point on the chart in the back of Lily's classroom.

And *that* night the little girl who had locked herself in the bathroom was all but forgotten.